Erotic Adventures of Annie and Mr. A

By: Annie Goodman

"The only pain in pleasure is the pleasure of the pain."

--Anne Rice

Part 1: Spanking stories

Chapter 1: The first time

Author's note: The story first appears in my novella, "First Times."

Most of my sex life, although great by most standards, had been predicated on leaning into my partners' fantasies and fetishes. I had never really given my own fantasies much thought. Each time I had sex and had an orgasm, I considered myself fulfilled. However, I had been dating someone pressing me to write fantasy stories for him. I wrote a story that leaned heavily into Anne Rice's Sleeping Beauty erotica. I hadn't read it in several years, but it had left a lasting impression, and I often conjured images in my head from that book during sex to add to my arousal.

My story left out any male servant parts and focused on a beautiful girl slave that was being considered for as a mate to the prince and had to pass through several submissive sex experiences. These included many situations of being spanked and paddled by both the king and queen. Mr. A read my story and asked me directly if I had ever been spanked or had an interest in being spanked.

My first response was an emphatic no. He and I had a great sexual relationship. I didn't want it going in some weird zone that we couldn't recover from. Also, we were two degreed professionals. How would this alter our power balance? Thirdly, I had never explored the pleasures involved with pain. Honestly, the entire idea was a bit terrifying. Just the idea, though, sent a ripple of pleasure through my loins.

He wasn't one to give up on an idea once it was recognized as a possibility. He started sending spanking memes. We watched The Secretary with James Spader and Maggie Gyllenhaal. He bought and read, and then suggested I read, "The Art of Spanking," by Milo Manara. I had seen The Secretary when it first came out in 2016, and I thought it was hot then, although I hadn't considered I might actually want to be spanked. I had even read Fifty Shades of Grey (just the first book) and wasn't impressed. But Mr. A was very persuasive and was working tirelessly and shamelessly to get me to comply. I finally acquiesced.

We settled on a weekend when neither of us had kids at home. He picked his house for the occasion. He suggested that neither of us have an orgasm the week leading up to event in hopes that we would both be fully aroused. He also had no experience with spanking and was equally, although excitably, nervous. We made out a few times during the week, but never the point of climax. He also wanted everything to be very formal and to present himself as somewhat of an authority figure over me. Rather than have me drive and meet him at his house, he picked me up, wearing a full suit and tie– looking very handsome. At this point in our dating, I had only seen him in jeans or shorts, never looking very formal. I wore a black mini skirt and a white V-necked T-shirt. He had definitely out dressed me. I looked more like a college student, and he was my finance professor.

In looking me over he said, "Annie, I am going to ask something of you. It might make you a little uncomfortable, but please, I'm hoping you'll comply."

"Okay?" I said, having no idea what he was going to ask. This whole idea that I had agreed on was a bit absurd to me.

"Could you not wear a bra to dinner? I know the T-shirt is white, but I'd love it if you could be daring enough to come to dinner braless," Mr. A asked in the same tone he might be asking me to take out the trash.

Oh wow. I wasn't even sure where we were going to dinner, but our town wasn't huge. It would be horrifying to be spotted out in a semi see-through T-shirt. My breasts were a solid and firm C cup. I often went braless at home, but not generally in public, and certainly not in anything white. Guessing my concern, he added, "Don't worry. We aren't staying in town. Our dinner reservations are in Columbus."

Columbus was safe. I felt confident I wouldn't run into anyone I knew. With some hesitation, I took off the bra and left it at home. I took one quick look at myself in the full-length mirror. The skirt was tight, showing off my toned calves and thighs from hours of the Peloton. I had chosen an orange wedge heel I purchased years ago during a trip to Italy. The white T-shirt was plain but also of a nice quality, although somewhat sheer. My breasts were firm enough that they were perky under the T-shirt, but my nipples were large enough that they could be made out just barely without the bra. I tousled my hair, hoping I could arrange it so that it hid my nipples. No such luck. They were going to be on full display tonight. He provided a huge approving smile as I walked out to the car, fully committed to this evening.

The restaurant lacked aesthetics but served great steaks and excellent wine. Action photos of their school's sports teams adorned the walls which were also painted in their school colors. The tables and chairs were simple and more of what you'd expect from a diner. But our waiter was professional and started us with a small loaf of freshly baked bread. Mr. A asked for a house Pinot Noir without looking at the menu or asking me what I preferred. He was in full dominant-mode. This was an entirely new side of him. Part of me was annoyed, but I was unmistakably turned on. My nipples had hardened against the shirt's cotton fabric, and I was hyper-aware of what this must look like. We enjoyed a glass of wine and a bit of the bread while waiting for the main course, which he had also ordered for each of us. He wasn't shy about staring at my breasts and asking how it was feeling.

"Sweetheart," he said, with a clear smirk on his face, "Would you be so kind as to run back out to the car for my wallet. I think I left it in the center console."

"You can't go out and get it?" I asked. He worked in a professional setting and had a secretary, so was definitely accustomed to being served, but this was a bit much.

"Sweetie, are you choosing to not obey me? That could turn into a consequence later," he said, rather coyly.

God. He was really playing this fantasy all the way through. Rolling my eyes, but complying, I headed towards the entrance, feeling several eyes on my chest with every step I took. I was very aware of each bounce each breast created as I walked. There was nothing to do but own the situation and stand tall. I realized his trick immediately–to humiliate me a bit and also so he could enjoy watching me make a solo entrance in the restaurant, walking towards him.

"Man," he said, shaking his head slowly, "I'm kind of hard already. You look amazingly hot."

Another eye roll from me, but I was feeling attractive, and believed that he was immensely turned on. The bit of role changing was working. The drawn-out dinner was making me more nervous, but he was savoring every minute of my discomfort. He ate slowly and provided a lot of small talk. I tried to offer that I wasn't super hungry, but he insisted that we weren't leaving until I clean my plate.

"You really are not very good at following orders, are you?" he teased with a quick wink.

That petite filet was feeling like a Porterhouse, but I begrudgingly ate mostly everything with his help in eating my greens and baked potato. The waitress suggested a dessert, but I beat him to the answer with a quick no thanks and request for the check. He didn't object, but my bit of defiance made me a bit nervous for what might come in my near future, given that I had already agreed to be spanked. On the way home, we again stuck to polite small talk with soft background music. When our conversation stalled, I realized he had even made a playlist of "naughty" songs for the occasion, including ``Spanked," by Van Halen, and "Sweet Head," by David Bowie. Once home, he poured us each a neat whiskey and we sat on his couch, me uncomfortably anticipating his next move. He took off his jacket but kept on his tie. As I sipped my whiskey, he began to assess my behavior throughout the evening.

"First," he began," I love your outfit tonight. Every guy in the restaurant and most of the women were checking you out. You should feel proud of how you look. Don't be shy of that. However, you broke some rules that are punishable. When I picked you up, I had to ask you to remove your bra. Do you remember? I asked, and you hesitated. That was disappointing," he said.

I held my gaze to him and tried not to smirk. I wasn't sure what to feel. His words were humiliating, and I felt like a schoolgirl being reprimanded by a stern teacher. Old feelings of wanting approval came back to me. I also recognized this was the man I had been dating for six months, who never once had raised his voice to me. I got it. We were role playing. It was just so different from what we had been doing. However, the game was fun. My crotch was responding very favorably to it, so I lowered my eyes and nodded that it was wrong of me to not immediately comply.

"At the restaurant, you also hesitated in getting my wallet, and you didn't want to eat all your dinner. Finally, you answered that we weren't getting dessert, which I really wanted. Who is in charge tonight?" he asked.

"You are," I mumbled.

"Excuse me? You must always speak up. Speak up and address me as Sir," he commanded with even more authority in his voice.

"You are, Sir," I said, a bit louder.

"That's better," he said, "But you have already earned a spanking for your actions this evening. Follow me upstairs please. Leave your drink on the coffee table."

He led me up his stairs, gently holding my hand as I trailed behind him. He had already prepared for the punishment by bringing in his desk chair from his office into the bedroom. He sat down and pulled me into his lap. His eyes stared into mine, asking with verbalizing a final consent. I nodded with a very slight smile. He lifted my chin and kissed me gently, then more determined, his tongue exploring with control over mouth, slightly biting my lower lip before moving to my neck. His hands explored under my shirt, squeezing each breast, but not asking that I remove any clothing. The kissing and petting were a nice transition. I felt loved. We were on good terms, no longer in trouble. But then, he directed me off his lap and I stood there awkwardly, not sure what to do next.

With one hand, he motioned for me to bend over his knees. Awkwardly, I laid over his lap, holding on to his ankles. He gently lifted my skirt to expose my panty-covered ass. He lifted the panties around my butt crack and caressed each cheek gently, but the weight of his hand on my ass was already creating a mound of moisture around my cunt. I was nervous he could already feel it. This was supposed to be a punishment. Not wasting more time, he tugged the panties back in place firmly smacked the left cheek then the right. The position was humiliating enough that the smacks seemed to carry more weight than they actually delivered. I remained still and relaxed into my punishment, thinking this wasn't nearly what I had worked up in my head. Then, without words, he pulled my panties down to my thighs, and delivered two more slaps to each side, hard and fast. I gasped an intake of air at the forcefulness of the slaps and immediately tightened my ass cheeks. The heat on them was immediate. I felt very much at his mercy with my bare ass exposed and my panties trapping my legs from moving much.

"Relax those cheeks, Annie," he instructed, "I'm just getting started." I willed my cheeks to unflex. He stroked each side lightly and slowly, sending an electrifying current throughout my body. He brought his hand down again. Two swift slaps on the left cheek then two more on the right where he rested his hand for just a moment.

"You keep tensing, and this session might get extended longer than you want," he teased. Again, I took a deep breath and with my air deflating my lungs, I again relaxed, ready to accept more. He again stroked over the newly formed welts he was leaving. The contrast between the slaps and the tender touch of his caresses was overwhelming. His free hand found a nipple and he tugged at it roughly, rolling it around between his thumb and forefinger which sent out an involuntary gasp of air from my mouth. Instead of more blows, he moved his hand between my legs, inserting a few fingers deep inside me. I was embarrassed by how wet I had gotten but bucking at his fingers just the same. I could feel his cock, hard against my belly. Just as suddenly as he had been teasing me with his finger, his hand slapped hard against my ass, in the middle this time, close to lips that were swelling for him. The pain was intense, but the pleasure was more pressing. He slapped that spot twice more before adding in my bottom edges of each butt cheek, leaving no trace of olive skin.

Abruptly, he switched his movements back to my nipples and cunt, working his fingers fast and hard inside me, expertly touching my clit and coaxing it to respond. My entire body felt a wave of pleasure as a deep orgasm washed over me. I moved my hips into his fingers, squeezing my hips and taking this pleasure without any remorse at later repercussions for my naughtiness. In a swift motion, he moved me off him and over the bed, spreading my legs with one foot, as far as my panties would allow then entering my cunt from behind. I felt waves of heat on my ass with every smack of his cock inside me and the pressure from his hands as he held my hips. He fucked in quick hard strokes without hesitation, until his orgasm came with force and an immediate satisfied release. This was the first of many successful spankings to come.

Chapter 2: Public spanking

Mr. A and I had dinner out regularly. He loved trying new restaurants and making an entire evening of it. He always insisted on the full meal experience, from appetizers to dessert. Most of our meals were eaten without our submissive play life being included. Sometimes though, he made a special request to play publicly. We had both had very busy weeks with little time for play or even vanilla sex. I was pleasantly surprised on this particular Friday when I received an unexpected text message from him. *I have missed your naked body this week. Feel like playing with me tonight?* I instantly went wet at my desk and looked around to make sure no one could see the crimson on my face. *Absolutely* I text back. Then he threw the curve ball- *I'm thinking about some public discipline. Still game?* My faced flushed a deeper crimson. This would be new territory for me, and a few hours' notice wasn't much time to think or prepare for what was about to happen. I took a deep breath in and replied, *Yes. I trust you. But getting back to work and putting my phone down. Home around 5:00.* I put my phone on my desk without giving myself more time to consider.

I drove home thinking mostly about work and other responsibilities, but when I stopped to get gas, there was a new text from him. *I laid out your outfit. Please be showered and dressed by 6:00. We have reservations for 6:30.* I nervously filled my car with gas, suddenly aware of all my nerve endings that had become heightened by his demands. Ninety percent of our time was spent in an equal relationship. The ten percent where I was his submissive was terrifying and exhilarating in one messily wrapped package.

When I arrived home, he was tucked away in his office, the door closed. On our bed, I found my outfit. The top was a pink-sequined tank top with a white cropped cardigan. No bra. I rolled back my eyes in annoyance. He knows I hate pink and shiny clothes. It only got worse. He laid out a pair of white panties, also in pink sequins. The back read "spank me." He also included a blue denim mini skirt with black heels, also not my favorite choice. The last item was a butt plug with a shimmery pink base. I was sensing a theme.

I showered quickly but took care to shave every reachable area, followed by a generous amount of body lotion. I accessorized with some tasteful jewelry that I was hoping would tamper some of the hideousness of the outfit.

Looking myself over in the mirror, I knew he would approve. The skirt was a few inches shorter than my comfort range, but the contrast between the skirt and the heels created an illusion that my legs were even longer than they were. It also accentuated the muscles in my legs. The sequined tank draped in a way that showed my breasts' natural cleavage with just a hint of my nipples. The cardigan was a bit of a buffer but did not hide that I was braless.

I walked downstairs to find Mr. A waiting for me in the living room. He was dressed impeccably. He wore dark tailored linen trousers that fit him perfectly with a pale pink dress shirt with a contrasting black floral design on the inside cuffs and collar. He took his time looking me over. The slight smirk on his face revealed his approval. He stood up and greeted me with a kiss that was gentle but hungry. He stared approvingly into my eyes as he held my face gently in his hands. "You look yummy," he grinned. "Are you sure you are ready for our night? I promise you will have fun even when you are hating it."

I did a bit of an eye roll but nodded my willingness to participate.

"Good. I have just one more thing," he said. "Please give me your ankle so I can add this to your outfit." I lifted my ankle up to him, craning my neck to see what he was doing. He placed a gold ankle bracelet just above my sandal strap. It said in simple cursive script, *Owned.* I gave him another eye roll but kept it on to please him.

"Great," he said, continuing to assess me. "Now, I need to inspect you to make sure you followed my orders. Bend over and touch your ankles, please." I stood where I was and did as he ordered. He hiked up my skirt to reveal the gaudy panties. "Very good. Let's see if you remembered the plug," he continued. He took his time pulling down my panties, only pulling them to my knees. He brushed his knuckles over the plug, sending a new gush of moisture through my pussy. He plunged a finger deep inside me "Oh no," he crooned. "Did I give you permission to be so wet already?" he asked.

"No sir," I replied back, getting quickly into my role as submissive.

"Hmm," he thought, while moving his finger methodically in and out of my pussy. He pulled his finger out and placed it in my mouth. "Suck your juices off my finger," he commanded. I suckled his finger as if I were sucking his cock, making sure I kept my eyes lowered. He yanked up my underwear. "Stand up then get on your knees, please," he commanded while unbuckling his belt and dropping his pants. His cock sprang out of his pants, and I obediently took it into my mouth.

"Good girl," he said. "Suck only my cock. No hands," he instructed. I put my hands behind my back to avoid being tempted to stroke his shaft or fondle his balls. I worked my mouth back and forth on his shaft, suckling the head of his penis, then absorbing his cock again, taking it as deep as I could without gagging. I knew better than to stop before being instructed. I worked into a rhythm of bobbing back and forth. He let out a sigh of pleasure, and lightly stroked my cheek. "That's enough for now," he said. "Stand up and head to the car."

On our way to the restaurant, he gave me his typical instructions and my last minute chance to back out. "I'm really looking forward to playing with you tonight," he began. "We will be dining at a nice restaurant with a lot of stuffy people. Your role tonight is to simply be my submissive. I will order for you. I will lead our conversations. You will be polite and accommodating. If I feel you aren't being a good submissive, you will be punished- when and where I choose to punish you. But remember you always have the choice to stop our play, and I will comply immediately. Are we still good?"

I squirmed a bit uncomfortably in my seat, the plug rubbing the insides of my butt cheeks, but nodded an affirmation to him. He smiled back, and we rode to the restaurant in silence, both anticipating the dinner. We pulled into a quaint neighborhood that I was not familiar with. Winding through a few blocks of groomed lawns and unique homes, we came to a row of neighborhood businesses, one of which was a French bistro.

Before stepping out of the car, he turned to me and drank me in one more time, very pleased with his selections for me. "One thing before we go inside," he started. "Take two fingers and finger yourself for just a second." His eyes did not break from mine as I did as instructed, putting my hand under my panties. My cunt was very tight with the plug crowded the space. I was still plenty wet.

"Good girl," he whispered, "Really work them inside you. When I tell you to remove them, I don't want you to wipe off your fingers. I want your scent on your fingers through dinner." I moved my fingers deeper as instructed, getting wetter with each thrust. My nipples hardened as my fluids released. The slight itchy fabric of the sequined tank top magnified the prickly feeling on each nipple as they hardened.

"Okay. Hands out of your panties. Let's go eat," he said in a more aloof tone as he jumped out the car with me trailing behind. The restaurant was very small inside with warm lighting and a cozy feel. We were seated at a booth near the back. I felt very out of place in my loud and tacky outfit that contrasted with Mr. A's sleek style. I tried not to stare at the other patrons but felt the fear that they were sizing us up, trying to understand our dynamic as a couple. I was praying no one could read my ankle bracelet or tell I was braless.

He started the dinner by ordering us cheese puffs and red wine to start. As he poured our glasses he said, "Thank you for having dinner with me tonight, darling. Each time you raise your glass for a drink of this delicious wine, please take a moment to inhale as you take in the scent of your fingers." He passed a glass to me and watched as I held it to my lips, watched me pause as I inhaled a bit dramatically, then took a nice sip. He chuckled quietly, nodding his head in approval.

We ate a wonderful main course of ratatouille. We settled into a nice rhythm of conversation, food, and wine. I almost forgot I was wearing ridiculous clothes and an ankle bracelet that said *owned*. I was enjoying how great Mr. A looked in his dress shirt, turned on by the ease by which he looked so comfortable. He was telling me a funny story about one of his clients, when he off-handedly changed the topic of conversation.

"I really do appreciate the outfit you are wearing tonight," he said.

"Um, Thanks?" I said. "It obviously isn't what I would have picked. I'm sure everyone thinks you picked me up randomly off the street tonight."

He looked shocked but amused at my comments. "Oh really? You look great. Everything about that outfit works for you. And you're lucky I didn't add a collar or necklace to the outfit."

I eyerolled again but nodded in agreement, taking another sip of what was left of the wine. "I'm sorry," he said, "but did you just drink without smelling your fingers?" he asked.

"I doubt there is a scent left on them," I challenged back.

"Did you confuse part of my instructions? I don't think I said to stop inhaling when you think the scent has dissipated. I also don't appreciate your attitude about your attire," he continued in a low voice. "These are disciplinary infractions that I just don't think that can wait until we get home," he said. Without saying more out loud, he picked up his phone and started typing. I took one last sip while sniffing my fingers, a bit louder than necessary, and waited for him to type what I knew would be instructions for me. Given that his initial proposal tonight was public discipline, I was getting very nervous. This place was tiny. There were at least three other tables filled with diners. My phone buzzed, and I dutifully ignored it as that was also an order of obedience while we were playing.

"Go ahead. Read your text," he said.

I've had a lovely dinner with you tonight, Sweetie. But, I think we both know that your obstinate behavior must be dealt with right now. You know better than to sulk about what I ask you to wear. Behind us are two restrooms that are unisex. You are going to leave your phone at the table and head to the restroom on the right. Keep the door unlocked and face the sink with your head bowed. I will be in shortly after you.

My eyes looked at him with shock, but I got up with raised eyebrows and went into the restroom on the right. I put my head down as told. I couldn't believe he had the balls to come into the restroom after me, to risk the chance that someone would see us both enter. I had to block out the idea that someone could be right on the other side. Despite my anxiety, I felt the wetness between my legs.

He entered the restroom without saying a word, but I heard the door click as he locked it and heard the hum of the overhead fan. "Come here quickly and bend over my lap," he instructed with a stern tone.

Mr. A was sitting over the toilet with a small red flogger in his hand, a new tool I'd never seen until this moment. "It's quiet," he whispered in anticipation of my question.

I bent over his lap, and he paused just a moment to stroke my ass, using his finger to outline the words *spank me* then quickly pulled them down and removed them before stuffing them in my mouth. He did not hesitate before bringing the flogger down on my tender ass, landing a blow on each cheek before pausing for a moment to gauge me reaction. My breathing had quickened, the flogger a total surprise. The first two blows stung horribly, but I was also still in shock that I was being spanked in a French Bistro bathroom. A series of blows were delivered as I squirmed and tightened my ass. I could feel my butt cheeks heating up. He used his other free hand to roughly squeeze my nipples under my tank top. They were already a bit sore from the rough fabric. He paused briefly to gently sweep the flogger's tails over each flaming cheek. I gasped from the pleasure/pain combination. I felt my knees go weak even though they weren't supporting me.

Whispering in my ear, he said, "Annie, Annie. I don't know what to do with you. This is your punishment for being bratty tonight. Yet your cunt is dripping wet. I'm going to flog you ten more times, harder this time. I want you to think about the bad girl you've been. I want you to decide how you can make it up to me once we are home. So, ten more strokes."

Without further warning, he released the tails forcefully on my cheeks, in-between my cheeks, and over my thighs while clamping down on one nipple with his thumb and pointer finger. The pain was intense. My panties muffled my grunts and cries as he showed no mercy with the last few blows. Finally finished, he allowed his hands to trace the red welts lightly in a loving gesture, then whispered in my ear once more. "I'm going to leave the restroom. You will remain in here until you have given yourself an orgasm. Then put your panties back on and we will eat dessert."

With three steps, he was out the door without so much as glancing back at me. I locked the door behind him, not wanting to remain in the restroom any longer than I had to, imagining now that everyone was wondering what was happening with us. I knew better than to lie and pretend I had masturbated. Mr. A would know, and my cunt was aching for relief. I took a paused moment to check out my ass cheeks in the mirror. They were bright red with some purple welts mixed in. The flogger had done its job at muffling the sound and bringing fewer blows with more power. I would be happy to not see that instrument any time soon. I closed my eyes and played with the nipple that had been spared abuse during my punishment. I used two fingers to satisfy the immediate throbbing between my legs, felt the wetness drip on my fingers, then quickly moved the fingers to my clit, rubbing in a circular motion as I relived the sensations of the flogging I just endured. Within seconds I erupted, bucking against my fingers and crying out into my panties still stuffed in my mouth as I felt a wave of spent desire wash over me. I removed the wet panties from my mouth, ashamed they had been used to mask both moans of pain and pleasure. I put them back on as ordered. The wet cotton material was rough against my tender butt cheeks. The plug also felt heavy in my ass, even more so after the release of my orgasm as everything swelled around it.

Taking a quick assessment of myself in the mirror, I was surprised to see that other than a flush across my face,

I look relatively unassuming. With just enough courage, I stepped out of the restroom and headed back to our table. Mr. A was calmly sitting at our table, eating what looked to be a delicious dish of creme brûlée. He commented as he watched me ease back down on the hard chair, my tender ass objecting, "Welcome back, Sweetie. I explained to our server that you weren't feeling up to dessert this evening, although I feel you already served yourself in the restroom," he paused and stared amusingly at the flush still spread across my face. "I'll get you home so that we can conclude our evening where I plan to devour every inch of you." He stood up and grabbed my hand to leave, his head held high. I kept my head bowed, very embarrassed and happy to never again show my face inside. He opened my car door and felt the new wetness at my crotch. "You know you loved every second of it," he confirmed with a smile. I did.

Chapter 3: First morning spankings

Mr. A and I were relaxing on the couch with a chill playlist playing through the Bluetooth speakers. He was sipping on whiskey, scrolling through his Twitter. I moved over and laid across his lap in only a T-shirt. "Please stroke my ass," I whispered, grabbing a pillow and getting comfortable. There was nothing better than Mr. A's hand stroking my ass cheeks. I craved the warmth his hand provided. We remained in that calm, relaxed way for several minutes while he sipped and stroked. I kept my eyes closed listening to the music. He finished his drink and reached over to put the glass on the ottoman, this time using both hands to explore. His strokes became more aggressive as kneaded one side while slipping his other hand inside my shirt, finding a nipple to tug and pull. I let out a soft moan, encouraging him to do more. He slipped two fingers in my cunt, and I moaned louder, arched my hips to swallow as much of his fingers as I could.

"Spank me lightly, please," I requested. I wanted to feel the transfer of heat from his hands to my butt cheeks. Without hesitation, he removed his fingers and brought his hand down on one butt cheek, not hard but with enough force for it to sting. I moaned an approval, kept my cheeks relaxed as he liked while spanking me. He slapped the other side then reinserted his fingers in my cunt.

"Man," he said, "I love how wet you are. You want more?" he asked.

"Yes, please," I replied. He continued with slow and methodical slaps, giving equal attention to both ass cheeks. His slaps built in strength, and my butt cheeks were flexing, fighting back against the sting.

"Play with yourself, Babe," he requested. "I want to see you buck in pleasure across my lap." He took my hand and guided my fingers to my clit. He kept one hand fondling my breasts and nipples, the other hand now lightly stroking the streaks of red he had just created on my ass cheeks. My clit responded immediately to my fingers. I lightly rubbed as I focused on the contrast of the extreme heat that was radiating off my ass with his now gentle touch. The next squeeze of my nipple sent me into a wave of pleasure that burst through all regions of my body. I cried out for several seconds, not wanting the orgasm to stop.

As soon as he felt my body begin to relax, he was quick to bend me over the couch and drop his pants just enough to free his cock and slide it in my cunt from behind. The roughness from his boxers and pants as they scraped against my ass amplified every hard thrust of his cock. He grabbed onto my hips and pulled me back harder and harder until he came deep inside me. Grabbing a blanket, he pulled out, sat down, and pulled me on his lap, giving me a lasting satisfied kiss.

"Hey," he said, "I have an idea to make our work week next week more interesting." My cunt immediately spoke to me with a light flex. His ideas always turned me on, even if they made me nervous.

"What are you thinking?" I asked, trying to sound skeptical.

"How about a full week of morning discipline? You service me before getting out of bed, then wait downstairs for your morning spanking before you leave for work."

"Oh, I don't know," I said at first. That sounded like a lot. "I'm not sure how this would benefit me at all."

"Oh Babe," he said in his sexiest voice, "You will be pleasured, either that morning or that evening– every day- same as me."

"I'd better have a drink with you to mentally prepare for this," I teased. We spent the remainder of the evening working out the details. Five days. I'd wake up at 6:30 and start by giving him a blow job, either to completion or stopping when he commanded. Then I would get ready for work. By 7:30 AM I was required to be on the living room ottoman, on all fours, ready to be spanked. I generally left for work at 7:45, so this didn't allow for too much to happen, I reasoned. Every day after work, he would be responsible for dinner and dinner clean up. The submissive play would only be in the morning and maybe some commands during the workday.

Monday

My alarm went off at 6:30. For just a moment, I forgot about our agreement, but looked at him and saw a small smile on his face. He hadn't forgotten. Without further delay, I pulled back the covers and nestled myself between his legs. His morning wood presented an already hard cock that I went to work on, beginning with very light kisses and licking his shaft. I kept one hand on the base of his cock while cupping his balls with the other. My fingers found the bulb of his cock, almost touching his asshole, and stroked lightly while my mouth suckled the head of his cock before taking him fully in my mouth. I switched my hands so that I was stroking the lower half of his dick while taking him deeply each time, keeping my mouth open and relaxed. A soft moan is the only sound or movement he allowed himself as my strokes became longer and harder down his shaft. My hand found the motion I knew he loved and worked rhythmically until I heard his sharp intake of breath, the only warning that he was ready to erupt. His final thrust in my mouth guided the semen down my throat, but I licked his entire cock and balls thoroughly to ensure I had all his cum inside me. Playing his part, his eyes remained closed as I got up to get ready, but the smile had fully spread over his face.

I showered quickly, anxious to be on the ottoman by 7:30. My work attire was business casual which usually meant slacks and some type of dressy shirt. I decided to stick with my normal attire, since I wasn't told otherwise. I had my car packed and ready to go for the day by 7:28. I made my way to the ottoman and found a vibrating easter egg– one of our play toys. He had left a note that simply read *turn on and place in your cunt.* I quickly took my pants down enough to slip the egg in, the vibration immediately creating a small gush around the device. I hopped up on the ottoman by 7:30. I knew to keep my head down and simply wait for Mr. A to come down the stairs. I heard his footsteps a short time later.

He walked around the ottoman, slowly watching me. I felt him kneel by my ear. He whispered, "Nice job this morning, Sweetie. That blow job was excellent. You were a very good girl." He stroked my hair, tucking a loose curl behind by ear. "But, I want you to spend your entire day remembering who you belong to. So, for that, you are going to get a spanking. Undo your pants for me, please." I unfastened my pants, and he swiftly pulled them down to my knees. He pulled my panties down next and placed a hand over my crotch, feeling for the vibration.

"Very good," he said. He stood to the side of the ottoman, bent over, and slapped each cheek four times each with quick, stinging blows. He stopped, walked to the front and ordered my tits out. I lifted up my blouse and pulled my tits out of their bra cups. He moved two bra pads against them, rubbery pads that had several small, hard bumps -almost like spikes- in them. We had used these before in play. They were not so painful that I couldn't take it, but also not my favorite toy.

"Get your tits on the ottoman so that they are touching these inserts," he ordered. Immediately, both nipples were erect and irritated. The aching sensation caused more gushing around the vibrator that was buzzing in my cunt. He went back to his position and smacked again, one ass cheek then another. He was creating a painting of welts in a short amount of time.

"On your back," he commanded. "Legs up." He moved the spiked inserts to my butt cheeks that were screaming against the dulled spikes. I wanted to rise up against them, but he put a firm hand against my tummy as he knelt between my legs. He caressed a breast as he pressed his tongue to my clit. He moved his hand from my tummy and gently tugged back on forth of the tail of the vibrator as he licked all over my cunt, devouring all the juice that had leaked out. He alternated squeezing each nipple lightly which sent new waves of pleasure through my body. I arched up away from the spiked pads as my climax began, crashing into his mouth, holding his head firmly against my cunt until the waves quieted. He pulled me up to him in a warm embrace, finally giving me the kiss I'd been longing for.

"You were amazing and delicious," he said as I was rearranging my clothes with three minutes to spare. "There is just one more thing," he continued with a sheepish smile on his face. "You did so great at following my orders. But that last bit, when you came, you did not stay on the spiked pads like I asked, did you, Babe?"

I wanted to protest but knew not to play into the bratty role, so I replied, "No, sir."

"You were so close to having an easy ride to work," he said. "But instead, I want you to wear these in your panties. When you get to work, I want you to silently FaceTime me and show me that you are just then removing them. Can you do that for me?" He asked. I nodded as he was picking them up to arrange them in my panties. The drive there was very uncomfortable. The heat from the spanking was amplified double by the spikes. I tried to sit very still so as not to exacerbate it. I felt it all over again with every bump in the road. I spent my entire driving thinking about my spanking and getting aroused again in spite of the pain from the makeshift punishment panties. I came into the office looking flushed. A few of my coworkers asked if I was feeling okay, but I mumbled something about just needing my morning coffee before slipping immediately into the bathroom. I Face Timed Mr. A as soon as I locked the door. He was smiling from his home office desk, legs kicked up totally relaxed. He held up a piece of paper that read, "You may remove the inserts." I propped the phone up against the toilet so that he could watch me remove the spiked inserts and put them in my purse. He quickly wrote, "I know you are wet right now. Have a good day at work." I gave him my best F-you stare and shut off my phone, smiling at just how wet my crotch actually was.

Tuesday

I overslept. I thought I had turned my alarm on for 6:30, but I popped up at 6:45. I started to move towards Mr A to get started on his blow job, but he moved a hand over my arm and said, "Too late. Go get ready for work and get on the ottoman. Wear pants with a belt."

I immediately felt a sense of dread for what I had done and what it would mean for me in just a few minutes. Still, I showered quickly and picked a pair of cream-colored pants that had very small belt loops. It matched well with a thin black rubber belt. I paired it with low heels and a tailored button down top. I worked for an insurance company. It was a friendly office, but we were expected to look nice every day. I busied myself enough with my morning routine that I had almost forgotten about what was ahead of me, but I did remember to get on the ottoman by 7:30. Today there was no toy. Mr. A came down in only his boxers, not looking at all happy. I knew our submissive play was something I could pull the plug on any time I wanted. But I enjoyed the game as much as he did, even when there were consequences for my actions.

"I'm sorry I overslept," I said, keeping my head down, hoping to soften his punishment.

"Oh Annie. Sorry is fine, but you know you must be punished, so that hopefully you won't forget tomorrow," he started. "Do you accept that you must be punished?" he asked. This was my cue to stop if I wanted.

"Yes, Sir," I replied, "ready to play."

"Good girl. Stand up so that I can see how amazing you look for work today. Very nice. Keep your head down, please. Now, take off your belt and hand it to me," he instructed.

I slipped the belt from my pant loops and handed it to him, head hung low, then placing my hands behind my back.

"Now, step out of those clothes while I make some coffee. I expect you back on the ottoman by the time my coffee is done." I removed my clothes and draped them over our couch, hoping to keep anything from looking disheveled. Naked, I got back on all fours on the ottoman, head down. I could smell the coffee brewing. He came back quietly, not saying a word to me. He walked slowly around the ottoman, drinking in my nakedness. He reached down and squeezed a nipple, rougher than normal, then kept moving. "Spread your legs wider," he commanded. I opened them as wide was they would spread on the ottoman. He pulled my butt cheeks away from each other, staring at my ass. He stroked each cheek lightly, put his finger in my cunt that was shamefully already wet and moved it around a bit before poking it in my ass.

"Push against my finger," he commanded. My asshole had wrapped around his finger. I pushed into it as much as I could without wanting to feel any more resistance in my ass. "Harder," he said, "I want you to rock back and forth. Fuck my finger." I started rocking back and forth, forcing myself to endure any pain I might feel. The nerve endings in my ass came alive and triggered a throbbing in my vagina. Just as I was starting to enjoy the anal finger fuck, I felt the first blow from the belt whip against my right butt cheek. He had doubled the belt, holding it with his free hand. I cried out and flexed hard, not expecting this spanking to start.

"Keep fucking my finger and count," he barked.

I quickly called out, "One," before the second crack came, and I cried out again but managed to call out a two. The belt hurt much more than his hands. I was sure welts were already forming on my right side. He handed out ten strokes before pausing to remove his finger from my ass and switched sides. He slid his finger in my cunt, adding a second finger. I was embarrassed by my wetness caused by the combination of pain and pleasure. He fingered me harder and harder thrusting his fingers as deep as they would go, and I felt a squirting gush spray over my legs and the ottoman. He pulled out his fingers and this time worked two fingers into my ass before delivering 10 strokes to my left side while I obediently counted. My ass was pulsating heat by the time he finished, and my cunt begged to be fucked. Instead, he moved back to my front and dropped his boxers.

"The quicker you make me cum, the quicker you get to work," he said as he motioned for me with one hand to put my mouth on his cock. It was very erect and ready for my mouth.

"May I also use my hands?" I asked, trying my hardest to obey.

"Yes. Sit up if it is easier for you," he offered.

I changed positions and sat on the ottoman, by ass rubbing against my spray mess from a few minutes ago, each welt stinging from the cool leather. I had little time, but I also didn't want to seem as though I was rushing. I started by stroking his shaft with my hand as I licked and nipped at his head. He was watching my performance, smiling in approval. I slipped my mouth over his head and bobbed as far as I could, opening my throat to go deeper, then puckered my lips tight around the base of his shaft before sucking all the way back up. He let out a moan of pleasure. I worked into his favorite rhythm, bobbing up and down with a mix of sucking tight and then barely sucking at all. I grabbed his ass and squeezed his cheeks, encouraging him to thrust in and out as he wanted. His ass cheeks tightened as his cock thrust hard into my throat, warm semen filling my mouth and sliding down my throat. I knew to swallow every drop rather than spit anything out or rinse in the sink after. My cunt was still throbbing for him, and I was hoping for release soon.

He sat beside me on the ottoman and lightly stroked a nipple so that it grew hard immediately between his thumb and finger. He whispered in my ear, "That was delightful, Annie. Thank you. But also, naughty girls don't get orgasms. You may dress and go to work. Do not get yourself off on the way or in the bathroom when you get there. Agreed?" he asked.

"Agreed," I sulked. He knew me so well.

Wednesday

We were up late Tuesday as Mr. A satisfied me multiple times in between great food and drinks. I wasn't surprised when my alarm went off that he would be very much still sleeping. I worked to position myself very quietly at his soft cock, ready to wake him up in the best possible way. Rather than straddle him, I moved to the side and got on my knees, butt in the air to bend over easily. Without using my hands, I consumed his cock in my mouth. Flaccid, it fit in easily. His body stirred just a bit and his dick twitched back just a little bit, already coming to life. I started by sucking lightly but firmly, growing his cock with each stroke until I struggled to take in his fullness. With the cock erect, I moved my mouth to his balls, taking one fully into my mouth and then the other, stroking his cock with a free hand. One of his hands found a nipple to gently caress and fondle while I worked on him. I licked between his legs, all around his scrotum, and back and forth on his stomach between the start of his shaft and his belly button. Each time he moaned in pleasure, I repeated my motion. Then I started the process over, my mouth covering his cock and sucking with more intensity.

He pulled away gently, "That's good for this morning, Babe. Go shower- oh and wear a skirt today," he instructed. I chose a pencil skirt and top with a wedge heel combo that helped me grow a few inches. When I went to the ottoman, I found a note. *Today's spanking will be in the dining room. Please remove your skirt and panties, make coffee, and be bent over the dining room table, tits and forearms on the table, legs spread apart.* I made coffee, poured him a cup, and arranged myself as instructed. The table was cold, and I felt awkward. I kept my face turned to one side so that I could see him make his entrance. I also took note of the mirror on the far wall in our living room. It was at a distance, but I could make out my naked body, fully exposed on the dining room table. I had pulled the blinds in the room but wondered if anyone could sneak a glance through the living room. My attention went back to Mr. A as soon as I heard his footsteps. This morning he was fully dressed and ready for work. He picked up his coffee and took a few sips while admiring me, a small smirk on his face.

He had a flogger in his other hand that he used to stroke my entire backside, starting at my shoulders and working all the way down to my ankles. I shuddered as my sensitive skin reacted to the strokes. He moved and sat in the chair closest to my face. He kissed my forehead, then said, "Your spanking will be over quickly today. I'm going to give you just ten swats with the flogger. I know you don't like it, and you were excellent with your mouth today," he rolled his eyes back in pleasure at the thought, then continued, "So, 10 swats. Then you will lay on the table and masturbate with the Hitachi wand while I watch and drink my coffee. When you've orgasmed, you will scoot down to me, and wrap your legs around my shoulders while I fuck you."

Instant wetness. I didn't love the flogger and didn't like being put on display, especially while masturbating. But his authoritative voice won me over every time. I braced for the flogger.

"Relax those cheeks, or I will give you five extra," he warned and began with a strike between my legs to start. The tails swiped over the backside of my sensitive lips, and I gasped as another stroke came down, this time on my left cheek. I winced but immediately relaxed, not wanting extra. I sucked in a breath of air and allowed my body to simply feel the sensations. I focused on the mirror and watched the tails fan out over my ass cheeks, creating a red painting against my olive skin. Mr. A was careful in selecting each spot on my ass to strike and set on creating a design, happy to leave his mark on me.

"Spread yourself on the table and fondle your nipples while I get the Hitachi," he ordered. I did as he ordered, wishing he had put down a blanket. My ass was throbbing, the memory of the stings alive. I began fondling my nipples, eyes closed. They were instantly erect as I tugged at them while rolling them between my fingers. I heard the Hitachi wand as Mr. A lightly pressed it to me vagina. I flinched from the hypersensitivity of my clit, not yet ready for its vibration.

He moved it to my hand and said, "I can't wait to watch." I kept my eyes closed but heard him sit in the chair nearest my crotch, heard him sip coffee. I refocused on my body. I continued stroking my nipples while holding the wand against my cunt, not directly on my clit. I slowly moved it north, closer and closer to the swollen gland that was screaming to be stroked. I lightly moved the wand against my sweet spot, forgetting about Mr. A watching. I bucked against the wand as my body exploded against it. I let out a scream of pleasure. Every part of my body was electrified. Mr. A brought me back to awareness as he tapped lightly on my foot, directing me to scoot towards him. He had already pulled down his pants. His cock was out, ready to enter me. I threw my legs around his shoulder as he slid in, anxious to share in the ecstasy. He fucked hard and fast. Each thrust bumped against my sore ass. Each thrust hit against my throbbing clit. I moaned and gasped at the intensity of the session. He came hard, his face crimson with pleasure as he held his breath and grunted as his orgasm shattered into my body. We basked in those few seconds after, relishing the calming effects of both orgasms. Then he pulled out of me and toweled off.

"Hand me the towel please," I said, smiling up at him.

He smiled back, "Oh Sweetie, I am surprised at you. You know I'm going to want you to wear my cum in your panties all day." He raised his eyebrows at me as he held my panties up, watched as I put them on without wiping away any juices from either of us.

Thursday

I woke promptly at 6:30 to perform my daily blow job on Mr. A but was met with an empty bed. Just as I was getting up to go to the bathroom, he came out of it wearing his robe.

"Good morning," he said, a cute grin on his face. "I thought we could hold the entire session in the bathroom this morning. I'd like to help you get ready for work."

"Ok…" I trailed off, not knowing how to react. But he was already turning on the water for us. Our shower was one of the highlights of our house. We had it completely remodeled when we moved in. It was a walk-in shower with dual shower heads, producing perfect water pressure. Each shower head had a handheld option. We were not strangers to shower sex but not typically in the morning when we were getting ready for work. He stripped off his robe and stepped in, so I followed suit. I picked up my loofah and started to scrub my body, but he took it from me.

"Here, let me wash you," he said as he began scrubbing my front side while kissing me. He scrubbed my arms, my belly, my breasts. He gently moved around my pussy before motioning for me to turn around. I let out a sigh of pleasure as he scrubbed my backside. He knelt on his knees to scrub my legs, pausing to kiss my ass cheeks and slid two fingers into my cunt. I steadied myself with two hands against a wall of the shower, not trusting the weakness I felt in my legs. My arousal grew quickly as I pushed against his fingers, eager for more. He pulled his fingers out as if it were part of washing me. Next, he squirted a dab of hair wash in the palm of his hand. He scrubbed my scalp with the perfect amount of pressure and directed me back into the water to rinse. He combed conditioner through my hair then kissed me again and directed my hand to his hard cock which I stroked before he motioned me to get lower. I dropped to my knees and cupped his ass with my hands while I brought his cock fully in my mouth, the water adding a sensual element. I devoured his scrotum, cleaning every inch with my mouth and tongue. He spread his legs and stepped for enough so that I could service that area closest to his anal opening.

"You're so, so good at this," he encouraged as I worked my way back to his cock, stroking and sucking it until he motioned for me to get back up.

"Time to rinse your hair," he said, indicating he was not interested in getting off yet. All rinsed, I stepped out of the shower, quickly wrapped my hair in a towel and used a second towel to dry the rest of my body, knowing the spanking was still in front of me but not knowing what more he had planned. I headed to our closet to choose my clothes for the morning, but he tapped me on the shoulder with my hairbrush. He was back in his robe.

"Come sit on this stool in front of me, so that I can brush your hair," he said. I fashioned the towel around me and took the other one off my head and sat in front of him. He brushed through all my tangles very lovingly. The bristles felt wonderful along my scalp, almost massage-like. I completely relaxed into his care of me.

"Today's spanking isn't because you've been naughty," he said as he brushed. "In fact, you have been quite wonderful this morning. Today's spanking is to remind you who you belong to, who you serve. Is that okay with you?" he asked.

"Of course," I answered but tensing up a little as I began to mentally prepare for the spanking after so much pampering.

"Very good," he said, "All done with your hair. Up off the stool and over my lap," he ordered as he sat on the side of our bathtub edge, hairbrush still in hand.

"You are using the hairbrush to spank me?" I asked.

"Quick thinker," he said, smiling while gesturing me down on his lap. "Towel off, please."

I removed the towel and bent over his lap, holding on to his ankles for balance. Using the backside of the hairbrush, he smacked each cheek three times each before stopping to lightly run his fingers over my ass cheeks. I took a deep breath in and out, steading myself for more blows. Four more were delivered quickly, and I could feel my cheeks reddening.

He paused again, finding my right nipple to play with then worked the handle of the brush into my cunt, knowing I'd be wet, moving it back and forth as I immediately moaned in pleasure. "That's a good girl," he whispered. "You are mine to pamper and mine to mark. Is that correct?" he asked as he continued to fondle me.

"Yes," I replied. "I am forever yours."

"Good," he replied as he removed the handle and stuck it in my mouth. "I'll finish with my hands. I want you to suck on that handle- taste yourself while I go one more round." He spent the next 30 seconds in an old-fashioned paddling of quick slaps on random ass cheeks as I bobbed against him, crying out in a muffled voice and trying to hold on to his ankles. I could feel my crotch pulsing from the hairbrush. My ass cheeks were burning wildly and throbbing. I could feel his hard cock rubbing against my belly, knew his excitement was growing as he delivered the blows, leaving his mark on my ass. He stopped the spanking abruptly, bent me over the tub and entered my cunt from behind, anchoring me with one hand on my tit and the other on my front side, my clit aching against his palm. His thrusts were quick and hard, his need for me evident. I had my hands over the tub, holding on, my legs in a locked position on the floor. In just a few thrusts he came deep inside me with a large, satisfied grunt, his body heavy behind me. He remained motionless behind me, but his hands continued to move. One circled my nipples, squeezed just enough to cause simultaneous pain and pleasure. The other rubbed my clit in a circular pattern. I pushed into it, loved the feeling of the heat on my ass against the rough hairs of his thighs. I bent my neck back against his chest and froze with arched hips as I climaxed long and hard, crying out in full approval of our session. I happily dressed without any clean up.

Friday

Friday morning Mr. A's cock was hard and ready for me to service when my alarm went off. My morning meeting was canceled, and I had a bit more time to play this morning. I decided to take my time with his blow job, to tease out his desire rather than bring him instant gratification. I straddled him with my ass on his stomach, legs tucked up behind me as I bent to receive his cock. Instead of going down, I started with feather-weight kisses on his cock then moved to more light kissing around his scrotum. My hands barely touched his cock, even as it arched to meet me. I licked the head of his penis as lightly as I could which resulted in a low growl from his mouth. I could tell he was enjoying the sensory deprivation. His hands moved to my hips, and he massaged my ass cheeks while I continued to lightly stroke and play with his cock, treating it like an appetizer rather than the main course. I licked every sensitive spot I could find; spending double the time each time he jumped or moaned. His fingers found their way inside me just as I tightened my lips around his cock, finally giving him full pressure. He finger fucked me as I fucked him with my mouth. Fluid gushed from my cunt as his fingers ramped deeper and deeper, our sheets a mess. I moved out of his fingers to switch the focus back to his cock. I transferred all of my arousal to taking him passionately into my mouth, not stopping until he was fully satisfied. I dutifully swallowed all his cum then continued to lick his cock clean before escaping to the shower.

I was surprised to not find him in bed when I finished getting ready. I came downstairs to find him drinking his coffee at the kitchen table.

"Do you want me on the ottoman?" I asked.

"Nope," he said, "Want some coffee?" He got up and poured me a cup. I sat down across from him, still with a few minutes to spare.

"Thanks," I said. "So, this is our last day…" I trailed off.

"It is," he said with a grin, taking another sip, looking completely relaxed and satisfied. I took another sip as well, waiting for his next move.

I finally stood up and started walking towards the garage. "Well, I should be getting to work," I said. He walked behind me as if to give me a kiss at my car. I opened the garage door and put my things in the passenger seat. He hit the garage door button again, stopping it halfway up.

"Today I thought it appropriate to spank you at your car, just before you are driving away," he said.

I looked towards the garage door. It was a beautiful Friday morning. People regularly walk by our house; it is a big neighborhood.

I saw his plan, immediately felt a ping of fear in my chest as I thought about being spanked in front of my neighbors. "You plan to spank me publicly?" I asked.

"Not publicly, Sweetie. Just semi-privately. Come here," he motioned. He was standing at the front of the car. He pulled me in front of him, gazing towards the driveway. "See, from here, you will be able to see out. But a walker would have to come up our driveway and look under the garage door to see what we are doing. It's perfectly safe," he smiled. He put a hand up my shirt, moved my bra, and caressed my breast, fondling my nipple, holding me from behind while I thought about it. He used his other hand to pull my panties down under my skirt. "Are you still wet from this morning?" He asked as a finger slipped inside me. "Ah, I see that you are. Naughty girl. You need this last spanking. Lean over the hood, please," he whispered. I did as I was told, blocking out the sounds of my neighbors walking by.

He tugged my skirt down and placed it on the car's hood beside my face. My panties were still halfway down my thighs. "Shh, don't make a sound," he advised as he started his final spanking. He struck over and over again without talking, one slap after the other. I tried to not tense up, but I kept grinding into the car trying to move from his hand. My clit rubbed against the front of the car, arousal radiating around my cunt. I couldn't see who was walking by, practically holding my breath to not be heard. He put his fingers back in my cunt, confirming the pleasure his slaps were creating despite the pain as I was squirming away from.

"Naughty, naughty," he whispered, again. "You look for pleasure even when being punished. I'm going to give you ten more smacks, harder for your final ones," he said as he brushed a kiss on my neck. I silently counted ten more whacks focusing on controlling my breathing. "Good girl," he said, "I'm all done." Mr. A immediately began lightly stroking my ass, electrifying every welt that was rising up. Chills ran through my spine at his sensuous touch. He bent over and planted several kisses on my ass as well, fingered me one final time and then pulled my panties back up over my hips. He picked up my skirt and said, "Go ahead and get dressed then get in your car."

I did as instructed, knowing my panties were already getting soaked from my juices. As I sat down he said, "Now. kick that seat back and relax. I'm going to join you on the other side." I laid the chair back as he did the same on. "Play with your nipples," he whispered as he moved his fingers over my clit, gently rubbing in a circular motion. I closed my eyes and arched my hips to him, my ass on fire, my nipples erect. I bit my own shoulder as I muffled a cry of pleasure, my orgasm was almost instantaneous. Mr. A stroked my curls, ran his fingers down my cheek and lifted my chin up, kissing me, his tongue finding mine. He sighed as he pulled away, stepped out of the car.

"Annie. I love you. Have a great day at work," he said, smiling at me before walking back inside the house.

Part 2: Anal Stories

Author's note: Chapters 4 and 5 were first published in

"First Times," available on Kindle and in books.

Chapter 4: First anal play

I made it through several years of a marriage

without any anal play. After my divorce, I

dated several men who never mentioned anal. Eventually

though, I found myself involved with someone that

preferred anal sex to vaginal sex. He put no pressure on me

to engage with him in any type of anal play, but I felt game

to explore this unchartered territory of my sexuality. Once a

week we'd establish a play date where we'd experiment

with all things anal with no hurry to get to the finale of

cock in ass action. Baby steps. For our first anal play

session, he suggested starting with dinner and drinks at his

place. I spent double the time getting ready that evening.

It was more than deciding what to wear. I didn't know how

to prepare "down there," in that very restricted area. I

wasn't comfortable talking to anyone else about something so taboo. I had been shaving my pussy for a while but hadn't really thought about my anus. Should I try to shave it? I took a nice hot shower and decided shaving was probably preferred. I tried to get into a wide squatting position and run the razor around my asshole. Feeling around with my finger, it seemed fairly smooth. I was half-tempted to slide my finger in and feel around but couldn't bring myself to take steps without him. I lathered myself with moisturizer and selected what I hoped was a sexy outfit– a semi-sheer button-down shirt, black corduroy mini-skirt with tall black boots that had a heel just high enough to bring me closer to face level with his 6-foot frame. I spent just a minute more scrutinizing the look in my full-length mirror and gained some confidence that the outfit was definitely playing to my assets. My toned legs were the focus with my breasts coming in second, as I had decided to go braless. The top did not hide the outline of my nipples but was not so sheer that you could make out much more. I only lived 10 minutes from his house, but 10 minutes was enough to amp up my anxiety over trying out new sexual terrain. My crotch was throbbing with anticipation. I had to fight the urge to caress my clit as I was driving.

He greeted me warmly, with a boy next door smile that helped to pat down some of my nervousness.

"I hope you are hungry," he said, "I might have prepped too much chicken. Also, I just opened a bottle of wine. I assumed tonight would be a wine night," he said with a hopeful look on his face as he led me to his back patio, handing mc a glass.

"This is perfect," I said as I sat in a wicker outdoor chair and took a large sip of the wine. It was a crisp October evening. With the outdoor heater, it was perfect for enjoying an outdoor meal. The wine immediately warmed my insides. I was actually planning to eat light tonight, not knowing what eating could do with anal play happening soon after dinner. We weren't on "expressing gas in front of each other" terms yet, let alone pooping near each other! He kept the wine flowing and the conversation going which helped distract my thoughts. We lingered a bit with another drink after dinner. Eventually, the time to play was inevitable. My anticipation was electrifying. I felt like I had just reached the front of the line for the tallest, most daring roller coaster– excited but also dreading the unknown aspect.

"So baby," he murmured in my ear as he bent down to kiss me lightly, "Are you ready to play with me?" His playful brown eyes were dangerously challenging. He exuded confidence.

"Lead the way," I said back, hoping to sound just as confident.

To my surprise, instead of leading me to the bed, he led me to his bathroom that had a garden tub with jets.

He had set candles around the tub and had Eucalyptus bubbles ready to pour into it. My anxiety was melting into simple trust for this man.

"If you want to fix the water and bubbles to your level of comfort, I'll pop open another bottle of wine and select some music," he suggested.

The hot water brought on a calmness that intermixed with the sexual energy present. For a long time, we just sipped wine and talked, but slowly he began stroking my body as we talked, taking his time to linger in spots or knead deeper in other areas. He ran the backside of his hand down my chest, grazing my left nipple which instantly shot sparks through my body. I moved over to sit on his lap, grabbing his face and pulling his lips to mine, feeling overcome with desire and yearning to explore. We moved from the tub to the bed, drying ourselves just enough. Despite my nervousness, I was eager to please him. I worked my way to his cock before he made his move. We had been together enough times that I had become an expert at handling his dick.

I started by slowly licking his shaft, making sure to cover all sides while also using one hand to stroke him and the other to lightly cup his balls. My tongue and cheeks sucked and licked at his head gently but firmly, allowing myself time to appreciate the smooth feel and to recognize the desire that was building. Taking my time, I decided to pull him deeper in my mouth but with very light pressure, moving his cock in and out as much as I could take. My goal wasn't to bring him to climax, so I moved around his cock a lot, giving equal attention to all of him. I spread his balls from his inner thigh and licked hungrily at each side before suckling each ball while also stroking the very lower part of his shaft that reaches his rectum. He moaned his approval as I worked my way back to his cock, this time taking a rhythmic mouth and hand approach that would most assuredly cause him to erupt if I kept it up. But he wasn't after a blow-job completion. With just a bit of hesitation, he pulled me away from his cock and back up to his face so that he was once again in control of the session.

We started making out again with a lot of heavy petting and stroking. I noticed that he had set out a few items on his nightstand in preparing for our play session. But to begin, he started with simply his pointer finger. Smiling over me with lots of reassurance, he put his finger in my mouth and said, "Get it nice and wet sweety. Time to get started."

I sucked his finger, trying to give it ample wetness. He slowly removed his finger from my mouth and again put his lips over mine, kissing them gently and using his free hand to fondle my nipples. His right hand moved between my legs, wedging his finger to the base of my asshole. He gently applied some pressure before pausing to gauge my reaction. I worked at not tensing my ass cheeks. Deep breaths, I told myself. He kept going and moved his finger gently but forcibly into my ass. I was immediately amazed at how tight I was but also at how many nerve frequencies were responding to just that little bit. I felt completely unable to move but also very alive. My cunt was pulsating, even though it wasn't the primary target. For several seconds he did nothing more than just keep the pressure of his finger inside me while continuing to kiss and fondle me. Eventually, he pulled his finger out and smiled his approval before reaching over me to his nightstand for something more substantial. My eyes grew wide as I saw him choose an enormous bulbous instrument that was shiny and silver with some bedazzling at the end in the shape of a heart.

"This is a butt plug," he quickly explained. "They make them in all sizes, but I thought we'd start small."

"This is small?" I said, completely surprised. "It is huge. How is this going to fit inside my asshole?"

"Shh. Trust me. It will slide right in. And if you don't like it, we can stop any time." Feeling brave from the wine, I nodded my consent.

Looking directly into my eyes, he took on the role of a sex instructor, of sorts. I found his voice intoxicating. My willingness to please him overrode my anxiousness. He stroked my hair and said, "I'm going to have you turn over on your stomach. You need to get in an ass up position with your tits touching the bed. By doing this, you will be exposing your ass to me, so that I can insert the plug. Can you do this for me, babe?" he said so gently but firmly.

Nodding, I flipped over and positioned myself as instructed. I tried to not think of the vulnerability of my position, but I had not felt this vulnerable in bed, ever. I closed my eyes and waited. I was slightly startled by the feel of cold lube as he delicately rubbed it around my ass, including the thin skin above the sphincter.

"Hold very still," he commanded. "This will feel tight. It might even burn just a bit, but you'll settle into it, I promise." With those words, I felt the cold tip of the plug press against my anal opening. He applied firm pressure while spreading my ass a bit with his hands. My anal opening went from having some push back to sucking the plug in with my cheeks almost covering it up entirely. I had an involuntary intake of breath as I felt the plug's fullness. It stimulated brand new nerve endings that weren't sure how to react. Part of me wanted to yank it immediately back out, but a bigger part was committed to knowing the full sensation. He lightly patted my butt and whispered, "You're a pro, Sweetie. That went in very easy. Your ass is beautiful."

I rolled back to my back, and we resumed making out. His swollen cock convinced me the plug in my ass was a turn-on for him. Within seconds, he covered his mouth over my clit. My vaginal lips were swollen and ripe. I was so wet that with his mix of saliva, it was almost too much.

One of his hands pulled a nipple aggressively while his

other hand gently pressed against the plug. My orgasm

came fast, without warning. I was a current of energy, the

plug the primary conductor.

I dropped to the floor and motioned for him to sit at

the edge of the bed, so that I could reciprocate. The plug

was still firing up my ass as I went down on him again,

harder this time with greater purpose, I used one hand to

stroke him as I kept my mouth open wide with my tongue

licking everywhere. I could feel his orgasm building as I

gently pressed and massaged his balls. When I knew he

was almost there, I changed my pattern to just my mouth

bobbing up and down, allowing his cock to guide the pace.

He let out a powerful moan as his cum worked its way

down my throat and chest.

He pulled me back up to the bed, cradling me in his

lap, stroking my hair again, not seeming to mind the cum

all over me. "That was amazing. Are you sure you don't have experience with this?" he teased.

"That was intense, so um- No. It was a bit like facing a fear and realizing there wasn't a reason to fear it. So, I think I'm game to do more," I confessed. "But also, are you going to take this plug out of me?" now feeling it as a bit uncomfortable.

He looked at his watch and said, "Fifteen more minutes, Babe. Your ass is being trained to take my cock. Let's have an after-sex drink while you finish your required training." Smiling, he led me back downstairs in just the butt plug and a shirt of his to the couch where we enjoyed a night cap. The plug wasn't comfortable as I sat with him, but I enjoyed knowing its purpose and thinking about our next steps. Totally worth it.

Chapter 5: First anal sex

Our anal play sessions became a weekly ritual that I came to enjoy. I found them challenging in that they always tested my sexual limits. On this Wednesday, I arrived expecting our normal routine of dinner, drinks, and play. He greeted me at the door with whiskey rather than wine.

"Hi," he said with a warm kiss, as he held out a whiskey glass to me.

"Hi," I said back. "Whiskey, huh? This is a change."

"Yes. I'm very excited to play tonight. I thought we could enjoy this drink and have an early play session before dinner. Are you okay with that?"

"Sure," I agreed, not quite sure where his plans were headed. The whiskey was good. The first sip warmed my insides and felt like a long sigh was running through my body. I closed my eyes, appreciatively.

"Blackened," he said.

"Blackened?"

"The whiskey. The name of it is Blackened. I rarely bring it out, but it seemed appropriate tonight," he explained.

I couldn't imagine what plans he had for our play sessions– didn't want to imagine. The whiskey did its job at clearing my head and putting me in an anxiety-free relaxed state. When our glasses were empty, he grabbed my hand and led me upstairs. Still standing, he stroked my hair back from my face and began kissing me, softly at first, but building to an eager hungriness. I could feel his cock grow beneath his jeans as he pressed into me. "Tonight, I thought we'd mix it up, do things out of order, if that's okay," he said again.

"What did you have in mind?" I asked.

"For starters, get undressed for me, and lay on the bed," he instructed quietly but confidently, his voice husky with longing. He made no moves to remove any of his clothes, still dressed in slacks and a nice buttoned-down shirt.

I stripped down slowly, hoping to draw out the moment. His eyes were fully focused on all parts of me. His full desire on display was my power over him. I cherished the moment. He kept his stare fixed on me for a few more seconds as I waited for him on the bed. Then he laid beside me on his side, me on my back as he kissed me slowly and fully as he stroked my body with his fingers, awakening the skin on my arms, nipples, belly, legs, and finally, my crotch. His mouth covered each erect nipple as he teased them into firm erect points. His hand worked its way between my crotch as he explored deep inside my vagina. My hips arched up to his finger fucking. I was anticipating his lips on my clit and couldn't wait for the sweet release of my orgasm.

"Please turn over," he said quietly as he unclamped from my nipple. He kissed my belly and lightly grazed the clit. "I am going to insert the next sized butt plug, and you are going to wear it during dinner tonight," he declared sheepishly, his smile daring me to disagree.

I rolled over, ready to receive the plug, but also hoping he'd put his mouth on my clit after it was in. He reached into his bed stand and pulled out a little black velvet satchel. He shook out its contents- a plug that appeared considerably bigger than the one we had been playing with. This one had a purple crystal at the tip, but flattened and circular. "Ass up high," he instructed. He began by lovingly caressing and kissing each ass cheek, moving his hands down each slope slowly, using his thumb to caress my cunt lips as he swept his fingers down the backs of my legs and then back up to my ass again. I heard him suckling on his own fingers before inserting first one, then two fingers into my ass. The sensation of being full amplified the throbbing in my vagina and the dull ache in my clit as I desperately wanted to get off. My nipples were still erect and rubbed lightly against the sheets. I was aware of so many sensations happening. It was close to a sensory overload, but I was fully on board to be challenged for more.

"Keep your tits down and use your hands to spread your ass cheeks," he instructed. "Keep it relaxed as I push in the plug."

Awkwardly, I spread my cheeks and focused on deep breaths. The first touch of the plug was cold and startling. He spread some lube directly around my asshole, working it around the perineum and some on the inside. He brought the plug back up, pushing gently but directly. I could feel my outer sphincter area burning as the plug was sucked inside me, but the burning subsided as the feeling of fullness took over. "Up we go," he said as he nudged me off the bed into a standing position

"We are going down to dinner now?" I asked, expecting still to have an orgasm first.

"Yes," he said. "I want you naked all evening with only the plug in your ass. We can finish after dinner," he grinned.

I knew that I could always say no to his plans, always alter what he was thinking, but it was a turn-on to be fully exposed to him while he was fully covered. He fixed us another drink before ordering Chinese from DoorDash. "You don't have to answer the door, but I find the idea that you are naked while I get our food to be highly erotic," he said before I could even offer an argument.

I squirmed quite a bit on the couch, shifting positions often to not feel the end of the plug that was visible. He made several requests that got me off the couch so that he could see the plug sparkle as my ass cheeks contracted back and forth. I barely remember eating; I was so fixated on having the plug removed and on finally getting off after being edged so close to an orgasm. I was appreciative of the whiskey's warmness, as it helped me to appear somewhat composed. I glanced in the mirror that hung adjacent to his couch. We looked quite the contrasting pair. He was still dressed head to toe in his business work attire– gray dress pants, crisp blue dress shirt, a patterned tie that coordinated the outfit. I was sitting with my legs tucked under at this point, attempting to relieve the discomfort of the plug edging from the rim of my ass. In the mirror, I could see the faint tracing of the purple stone from the plug.

"Lay belly down on the couch," he said. I want to drink in your backside." He stood up and placed a blanket over the couch and motioned for me to lie down. I closed my eyes and tried not to feel over-exposed as I could feel his eyes staring at my nakedness. He knelt by the couch and placed his hands on me, starting with my back. He made faint circles with his hands and then worked his way down, fanning his fingers as they stroked downward. He paused on my ass, bent over with light kisses and then small bites and sucking all around my ass. He kneaded my butt cheeks with one hand as he worked his other fingers inside by cunt. I could hear his breath quickening, and knew his excitement was growing.

"Please take your clothes off," I suggested, desperately wanting his cock in my mouth. I didn't wait for a reply but unbuckled his belt as he removed his tie and started unbuttoning his shirt. I enveloped his cock as soon as his pants dropped, cupping his butt with my hands, and forcing all of him in my mouth. His cock grew quickly and I gagged reflexively as my limits were reached. I licked all over his balls, the tip of his penis, his shaft, my tongue circling all around. He pulled away with a smile and a small shake of his head.

"That's enough," he said. "Baby, it's time. Are you ready for my cock in your ass? I'm going to pull out the plug that has your asshole stretched and insert my cock in its place." He rearranged the blanket to the chaise lounge

part of the couch. "Get on all fours right here," he said,
directing me over. I moved as instructed, trying to not think
about what was about to happen but to let the experience
wash over me. He gently pulled the plug, and simply
whispered, "beautiful" before I felt his body behind mine.
He put one hand on the back of my shoulder as he used the
other to guide his cock into my ass. I gasped out a small cry
as I felt all of him inside me. He stood motionless for the
first several seconds, allowing me to drink in the new
sensations. I could feel his balls fall between my ass and
cunt, slightly pressing my skin. My cunt was pulsating,
keeping a rhythm to add a stimulating sensation. My clit
ached to be touched. I could feel my nipples grow hard
without any direct stimulation. My breathing was heavy but
controlled.

Slowly, he moved his cock in long slow strokes,
back and forth inside my ass. Each stroke was felt
intensely, but with no pain. It was a deep sensation that

created a desire for him to go harder and deeper. I rocked back into him, encouraging him to continue. He grabbed onto my hips and pulled harder and faster. His cock found its rhythm in my ass, stroking hard and deep. My cries grew louder as the intensity picked up until I felt his entire body shudder against mine. I felt locked into his body, tighter than I ever had with vaginal sex. He was motionless for just a moment before rearranging his hands to fondle my left nipple and slowly stroke my clit, his cock still inside my ass. The sensation of feeling pinned down by his cock in my ass adding to the sensualness of his fingers against my clit. My immobility created a strong wave of current through my body as I was unable to arch my body away from the intensity. My screams of desire were primal and raw. After what seemed an eternity, muscles began to relax, my breathing slowed, and the awareness of our positioning came back into focus. He stroked my hair and slowly started to disengage his penis from my ass, pulling out slowly. I flipped on my back and pulled his face into

me for a deep kiss of approval.

Chapter 6: Costa Rica

Mr. A and I had been having a wonderful vacation in Costa Rica. Every day was a new adventure between snorkeling, hiking in the rain forest, and sex at all hours of the day. We rented an AirBnb for the week in beautiful Manuel Antonio. The house sat high on a cliff's edge with spectacular views of the ocean below. Our veranda included a covered pergola and small pool, perfect for midnight dips while watching the sailboats below. We could hear other neighbors dotted around the cliff side but felt like we were nestled in our own outdoor playground. We spent most afternoons nude on our deck, lazily sunbathing with a good book and often pausing for sex whenever the mood struck either one of us.

On this particular evening, we decided to take advantage of the outdoor kitchen and grill steaks on our patio. We had spent the day enjoying a sailboat snorkeling tour and were both slightly sunburned from the day's adventures. I was enjoying a glass of wine and reading my

book on a lounge chair, my silk kimono robe floating over

my slightly burnt skin. Mr. A had changed from his pair of

swim trunks to a pair of boxers, opting to not put anything

else on for the evening. I lazily smiled over at him as he

began preparing the grill for our steaks. He walked over

and kissed the top of my head.

"You look sleepy," he said. "I'm glad we didn't go

out for dinner. I am guessing we'll be sleeping shortly after

we eat tonight."

"Um, most definitely," I said. "I can barely keep my

eyes open to read. Need some help?"

"Nope. Potatoes have been in the oven an hour

already. Steaks won't take long. Enjoy your wine," he said

and walked back to the grill.

Dinner was simple but delicious. Mr. A joined me

on a lounger as we poured ourselves more wine. As the sun

was setting on the water, all the lights from the sailboats

were coming to life, creating a firefly effect along the ocean in front of us. It was very peaceful. Instead of going to sleep as planned, we opened a second bottle of red wine, deep in conversation.

"Worst sex you ever had with anyone?" Mr. A asked with a playful look on his face.

"Literally any teen sex was bad sex for me," I laughed. "Why do boys think that rabbit fucking is okay?"

"Rabbit fucking? Really? I knew how to please girls as soon as I started having sex," he said with just a hint of cockiness to his voice. He certainly knew how to please a woman today, I thought, shrugging in agreement.

"Well, you didn't attend *my* high school. Only rabbits and their small penises," I added.

He laughed, "Oh, and now they all had small penises. I think you are trying to earn some brownie points," he said.

"New question. Your turn," I said, taking another sip of wine. "Where is the craziest place you have ever had sex?" I asked.

"Oh, that's hard. You and I have had lots of great sex in crazy places. So, if I don't count those, I'd say under the bleachers during a high school football game."

"What? That's disgusting," I challenged. "How did you get away with that and why– just what would possess you?"

"Lara Hines possessed me. She liked sex. One minute we were in the bleachers watching the game, and the next she was daring me to see what the game looked like from underneath. She slipped out of her panties and asked me how quickly I could cum. I most certainly became a temporary rabbit at that moment," he answered reflectively.

I just couldn't quite picture my partner fucking some young girl under the bleachers while parents and teens watched the game from just a few feet away. It was kind of gross but also kind of stimulating. I was amazingly tired, but I felt my pussy pulsate in response. I sipped more wine and untied my kimono, allowing it to fall open, exposing my breasts. I moved from the lounger to the teak dining table, sitting on the top surface rather than a dining chair. He followed without saying a word and leaned into me for a long kiss that created more stirrings.

"Pantyless, I see," he said as he brushed his fingers lightly over my lips.

"Isn't that our vacation rule?" I asked. "No underclothes while at the house?"

"Oh, it is, sweetie. I'm so happy you have granted me this wish all week," he said while fondling a breast. "I love the easy access to all of you."

I leaned back further as he played with my nipples, taking turns suckling them and weaving them around his fingers. The light breeze on my sunburned body amplified my nerve endings. I let out a soft gasp of pleasure. The wine had made me bolder but not less sensitive. I was going to cum as soon as he touched my crotch, which I didn't want to do yet.

I willed myself away from his touch and said, "Switch me spots, boxers off, please."

"I love it when you are bossy," he said as he stripped off his boxers and leaned back in the same manner. I sat down in front of him, placing my hands just under his thighs to lift his package off the table a bit, giving me full access. I planted my tongue to the very back tip of his anal opening and licked towards his scrotum, working my way around each ball. I could hear his breathe quickening, could sense his cock flexing. I knew he was silently begging me to get my mouth all over his cock. Not yet. I licked my pinky finger and worked it into his asshole, keeping it firmly in place while I suckled one ball, popping it out of my mouth and then slathering his ball sack with my mouth before sucking his other ball into my mouth. He moaned with pleasure and squeezed his butt cheeks towards me. Slowly, I removed my finger but pressed it on the hidden part of his shaft as I finally took his cock into my mouth, stroking with my hands and feeding my mouth. My mouth stroked rhythmically up and down several times before slowing around the tip of his cock and licking around the silky smoothness of the head, sucking harder until he gasped with approval.

"Bend over this table so I can fuck you," he said hoarsely. I knew he was close to exploding.

"Better idea," I said, moving to the railing that overlooks the other homes and the ocean. We could hear voices that carried in the air. There was music playing faintly from one of the sail boats. The evening was peaceful, but we weren't entirely alone. Being at the railing felt like being a part of the collective chatter around us.

Daring him, I said, "Please fuck me in the ass over the railing."

He pulled me in close for an urgent kiss, thrusting his tongue deep into my mouth. I held on as he teased my frontside with kisses. Two of his fingers plunged inside me, releasing juices that had been building. His teeth grazed over a nipple, suckling with an intensity that matched his fingers deep inside my cunt. I grinded into him, never tiring of how much I wanted his touch.

"Turn around and bend over," he commanded huskily. I bent into the railing, sticking my ass out as much as I could for him. He got on his knees and used both hands to spread my ass cheeks. He placed his tongue over the rim of my ass, licking lightly all around before plunging it into my asshole. My cunt throbbed with a dull pain that begged for more. He stood up and fingered my ass with one of the fingers that had just been in my cunt, slowly moving it back and forth before adding the second finger. I could hear laughter nearby, even heard the clinking of glasses, so I was betting they would be able to hear us if we got too loud. I wondered if our shadows could be seen from any vantage point. The thought made me want his cock inside my ass even more.

"Fuck my ass, now please," I asked, knowing he would be even more turned on by the request.

"Only if you play with yourself while I fuck you," he said. I nodded.

"Spread your cheeks," he ordered. I reached back and opened myself to him. He entered my ass slowly, allowing me to feel every inch of his cock settling into my ass. The feeling was that of immense fullness. It lit up nerve endings in all my sensual spots. I thought I might explode from the intensity if he moved at all. He played with a nipple as he allowed me to settle into the feeling.

"Touch yourself," he whispered.

I reached between my legs and found my clit. It was so hypersensitive at first that I had to pull away from it. I rubbed the area just above it for a few moments. He began moving inside of me, very slowly then settled back with his cock so tight in my ass that I could feel his ball sack pressed tightly against me as well. He tugged and pulled my nipple as I circled my clit very lightly. I could feel my orgasm building and squeezed harder against him. As soon as he felt me hold my breath, he began to move his cock again. My orgasm erupted as his rhythm quickened. The inability to scream out in pleasure heightened the intensity as he rammed his cock back and forth in my ass harder and harder, holding the edges of my hips to guide me back to him each time. My orgasm lasted several long seconds as I felt him release deep into me, grunting in pleasure but also keeping his voice level in check. We remained motionless for several seconds, basking in the feeling of being completely spent. I opened my eyes and was brought back to the present. I observed the sail boats across the water, the houses dotting the cliff, and wondered if anyone knew what we had been doing. He pulled out slowly as semen dripped out my backside, and onto the deck, its creaminess reflecting against the moon's lighting. I smiled up at him, kissed him with some lingering desire.

"One more glass of wine before bed?" I suggested.

"I'll pour if you grab us a blanket," he said, already reaching for the bottle. I spread the blanket over both our chairs.

"So, what's the best sex you ever had," I asked.

"This one time," he started, "I ass-fucked an amazing woman over the railing of a resort home in Costa Rica. . ."

Chapter 7: Champagne enema

Mr. A liked to experiment, and I was his muse. I was typically game to try most things at least once before I deemed them off limits. But some things were beyond my comfort zone. One such item was taking liquids into my ass. He had this fantasy of drinking champagne from my ass and had asked more than once. I had said no more than once. But here it was just a few days before Christmas with not much to put in his stocking, and there it was– a half-size bottle of champagne to celebrate the new year. And just like that, my willingness to try it opened.

Christmas morning always started peacefully. We weren't expected to be at my parents or his parents before noon, so the morning was ours to celebrate alone. Presents were great, but my favorite part was the stockings, which were always filled with surprises. Mr. A included a mix of naughty and nice in mine– jewelry from a local artist, my favorite candy, socks, a new novel, and in the boot of the stocking, a new glass dildo. It was beautiful with orange swirls intermixed into the glass.

"Wow–that is a big and beautiful dildo!" I exclaimed. "I hope we don't break it. I'm almost afraid to use it."

"Perfectly safe," he said. "We'd have to drop it on the hardwood to break it. I can't wait to see you fuck yourself with it." He leaned in and kissed me, pulling my face to his, his tongue taking its time exploring my mouth.

"You're up next," I said, presenting his stocking to him. He thoughtfully complimented each item he pulled out. I went mostly conservative– new workout socks, boxers, chocolate bars from a specialty shop, and hot sauce I had purchased from our trip to Costa Rica. Lastly, he pulled out the champagne. I had wrapped it in shiny metallic paper as well as concealed it at the bottom of the stocking. His face registered complete shock when he unwrapped it. He stared at me with his mouth agape, his eyes tripling in size.

"This can't mean what I am hoping it means?" he asked. I smiled and nodded, still not 100% sure but taking the dip. "Jesus Christ, sweetie. Oh my God. I.. oh wow.. I might be cumming a little in my pants right now. This is amazing. When?" He pulled me up for a lingering kiss of gratitude. There may have even been a tear in his eye.

"Well, we were planning to stay in for New Years," I suggested.

"Oh my God, yes. That is perfect. That gives me a week to plan this out," he said, kissing me again, before picking me up and carrying me to the couch. He hungrily devoured my mouth, his tongue exploring inside my cheeks and all around my tongue, his teeth biting my lower lip. His hands found my breast, squeezing and pulling. My nipple perked up as soon as his thumb grazed it. I yanked off my shirt, giving him full access to play with both nipples. He suckled one while fondling the other. I could feel his cock growing beneath his sweats, begging to get out.

He pulled my sweats and panties to my knees and thrust his two middle fingers in my cunt. "Fuck, I love how wet you are," he whispered as he fucked me with his fingers. They slid in and out easily as my hips rose to encourage more. "I need to taste you," he said as he repositioned himself between my legs. Both hands twisted my nipples aggressively as his mouth clamped down on the perfect spot, his tongue caressing lightly in small swirls before pulsing against my clit. As my orgasm built, I tried to pull away a bit to ease the intensity, but he pulled me in tighter, keeping his mouth clamped as I cried out in ecstasy. Waves of pleasure washed over me as he continued to lick me and hold me against him. He didn't stop until I was purring from contentment.

"Flip over," he commanded, his cock overdue for relief. I got up on all fours, and he guided his cock in my swollen vagina, still aching from my climax. I screamed out with every thrust as his hands guided my hips back and forth. He paused, pulled out, then repositioned in my ass. He entered slowly, allowing me time to absorb every inch of him. I let out a low moan of approval of the new position, flexing my muscles to squeeze all around his cock. He pulled back so that only his tip was in before ramming his shaft back inside me before repeating. My cunt throbbed with each thrust, aching as the swelling increased. I moved lower so that my elbows rested on the couch. My nipples rubbed against the rough fabric as he rocked into me, holding my hips.

"Please, fuck my ass," I asked, the slow rhythm torturing me. I wanted to feel his cock slam hard against every nerve inside my ass. He complied without hesitation, his orgasm building quickly with each thrust. He cried out loudly as his semen erupted. We took a few minutes to recover, before I glanced at my watch. We had just enough time to wish the parents a Merry Christmas.

The week passed quickly. We were both off work and had many little projects to complete around the house. "Do you want to know my plan for us on NYE?" Mr. A asked me one evening. Sometimes he wrote out a proposal for me to approve before we played.

"I'm already granting you permission to pour champagne in my asshole. I can't imagine you are proposing anything bolder than that?" I asked.

"Nope. That will be the crescendo of the evening. I didn't want to assume anything, though."

"Plan away," I said, not wanting to know what was in store for me.

We spent the first part of December 31st with friends. Someone had organized a lunch date. I decided to eat lightly all day, knowing what was in store for me later. We were very vague when asked about our evening plans. I mentioned I'd probably be writing out goals and just laying around. Mr. A confessed he planned to drink some champagne. My body tensed with nervousness at the thought of it. We were back home by 4:00. Each minute felt like hours, as I waited in anticipation of what that experience would feel like. I decided to hop on the Peloton for an hour to spend some of my nervous energy. When I got off the bike, Mr. A was waiting for me in our bathroom.

"There are preparations that need to be made before we start the evening," he said, holding an enema bag in his hand. He had only administered an enema to me one other time, and I knew what that meant. He was planning for ass to mouth with anal tonight. He knew I was very skeptical about his cock in mouth after it had been in my ass. This was our compromise. He had already made a bed of towels on the bathroom floor for me.

"Ok," I said. You want to do this before I shower?"

I leaned in and kissed him, letting him know I was completely his for the night, however he wanted to use me.

"Yes. It's best to do the enema before you shower, but I was planning to draw you a bath so you can relax before the next step," he said, kissing me back. "Get your sweaty clothes off and lay on the towels on your side," he instructed.

I stripped down and got in position. He had prepared a homemade solution that he found online for anal play. The red bladder and long nozzle were intimidating. He had brought in a chair to sit on while administering it. This procedure was humiliating to me, but he did it with such love and care, my emotions were all over the place.

"Pull your ass cheeks apart for me, while I stick the nozzle in your asshole," he ordered. The long tube felt foreign inside my body. "Relax. I'm going to start expressing the mixture into your ass. It should feel warm.

I'll try to go slow." I took some deep breaths and held it for several seconds, eyes closed as I felt the liquids fill my insides. He paused for a moment as the first dosage drained then squeezed the bag to release more. My stomach started cramping within a few minutes. He squirted another round before removing the nozzle. He put the chair back and sat down beside me on the floor, stroking my hair.

"Hold it in until you feel like you can't hold it in anymore," he said, "then head to the toilet."

"Okay. Right now, it feels like menstrual cramps–not at all sexy," I complained.

"You're doing great," he said, smiling at me with sympathy. "I know you don't like this, but this part is a turn-on for me. You still look sexy naked on the floor."

I growled quietly at him, not feeling sexy. I suddenly felt an urge to push. I held the liquid in another minute, squeezing as tightly as I could, before jumping up and repositioning myself on the toilet. I spent the next five

minutes squeezing out every ounce of liquid I could, mixed
in with anything in the lower part of my colon. I felt
confident nothing was left inside. Feeling much better, I
stepped out of the water closet to find Mr. A creating a
wonderful bath for me. He had lit candles around the tub
and added eucalyptus scented bubbles. I pinned my hair up
high on my head and stepped in, sinking into the water until
it was level with my chin. He handed me a glass of wine
and patted my head.

"Enjoy and relax. Take your time. I'll be
downstairs," he said. The bath immediately wiped away the
discomfort of the enema. I stayed in until my wine was
gone, and the water cooled. I let out about half the water
then carefully shaved every bit of hair from my ass and
vagina that I could reach. I drained the remaining water
then showered off the bubbles. I decided to wear a sexy
cocktail dress and heels to get in the NYE mood, also
applying makeup and fixing my hair as if we were going

out for the evening. When I came downstairs, I found Mr.
A reading on the couch, dressed in nice dress pants and a
button-down shirt and tie, looking very handsome. I
appreciated the like-mindedness. He was drinking bourbon
and had a second glass of wine waiting for me.

"You look amazing," he said, drinking me in with
his eyes. "I thought we'd relax with a drink together before
doing anything else."

"You also look very nice," I said, taking another sip
of the wine, grateful for the drink.

"I do have one early request," he said. He reached
into the top pocket of his dress shirt and pulled out a small
butt plug. It was all glass, similar to the glass dildo he had
in my stocking. "Would you allow me to insert this inside
your ass now?" he asked.

"Of course," I replied. "Do you want me to bend
over your lap?" I asked, "Do you have lube?"

"In my pants pocket," he smiled, producing a small bottle. I laid over his lap. He flipped up my dress and pulled down my panties. He squeezed a small amount on his finger and forced it in slowly, moving it back and forth. I gasped slightly at the wonderful familiar feeling, already melting for more of his touch. He pulled out his finger and replaced it with the plug, gently guiding it in. My ass resisted at first but then relaxed enough to suck it tight against my ass. He pulled my panties back up and lightly patted my butt.

"Thank you for indulging me," he said, smiling.

"Happy New Year," I said, lifting my glass to him, also squirming a bit to find a position that was somewhat comfortable. For the next hour we laughed, talked, and drank, completely relaxed. The plug created a feeling of fullness inside me that kept my nipples erect and my cunt wet.

When the last of my wine was consumed, he looked at me and simply said, "Ready?"

"Where do you want me?" I asked.

"Right back over my lap," he said, "I want to spank your beautiful ass so that it is red hot while I'm fucking it later."

Just the mention of his hand on my ass sent new warmth over my cunt. I laid back across his lap, keeping my dress on for now. He raised my dress back up, but kept the thong wedged between my butt cheeks, the plug sticking slightly out. He caressed each butt cheek lovingly before paddling me with his hands, striking firmly and evenly so that my ass was thoroughly red. The heat was intense as it throbbed from his blows. Without any warning, he flipped me over and began caressing my front side, massaging my nipples and clit simultaneously. As much as I wanted his mouth on me, my orgasm was already flowing as soon as his palm rubbed against me. He squeezed harder on my nipple and rubbed my clit in a circular motion as I screamed with release. Suddenly so spent with pleasure, I didn't care what he did to me next.

As he brushed back the curls from my face, he said, "If you are ready, I put more towels down on the kitchen floor. Please undress and get on all fours over the towels."

I leaned up and kissed him once more, still basking in the fullness between my legs. I slipped the dress over my head and unstrapped my heels before getting into position. Mr. A kept his clothes on for the moment. He walked over and fully inspected me, lightly running his fingers down my spine and ass, still emanating heat from the spanking. He gently pulled out the plug and set it aside. He picked up the bottle of champagne and popped it open.

"Happy New Year, Sweetie," he said, tipping the bottle in my direction. I'm going to pour a glassful into your ass, then when I say squeeze, squeeze as hard as you can into my glass, okay?"

"Let's do it," I said, wishing I was tipsier from the wine.

"It's going to feel cold, so sorry about that," he said as he started pouring in the champagne. The bubbliness burned as it went in, its coldness chilling my entire body. It was a sensation I had never felt before. I wasn't sure how I felt about it. Before I had a chance to ponder on it more, he said, "Squeeze!"

I could feel the champagne flute against my ass as I squeezed hard, praying the enema had worked. "Beautiful," he said, as I heard liquid drip into his glass. I squeezed once more, trying to angle my ass down more and heard more slip out.

"Perfect. That's good, Sweetie. You can stand now." He poured me a glass of champagne from the bottle. His hands were shaking a bit, the only indicator that he was also nervous.

"Cheers," he said, holding up his glass, "I love you, so much." We clanked our glasses together and he swallowed his champagne in one gulp, smacking his lips in approval.

"That was so hot," he said, shaking his head. "Bend over this table so that I can fuck you hard." I bent over, tits fully on the table.

"Face down too, please. We are going ass to mouth. I need your mouth ready," he instructed. He spread my legs further apart with his knee. Grabbing the funnel, he poured the last bit of champagne into my ass. I heard him unzipping his pants. He came around to my face and said, "Suck me for a second first."

I fucked him with my mouth for a few seconds, but he was more eager to put it in my ass. He bypassed my cunt altogether. The plug created an easy opening for him as his cock slid in. He placed his hands over my red ass as he pumped hard several times, groaning in pleasure. I screamed out each time. The slow burn of the champagne amplified every thrust. He pulled out suddenly and put his cock back in my mouth as he also controlled the intensity of the fucking. I wasn't giving him a blow job. He was fucking my mouth. His cock was so hard and smooth, I wasn't sure where he would choose to cum, but he pulled back out and put himself back in my ass. He slowed down a few strokes, allowing me to suck in a breath, before picking up the pace again, this time going deeper and deeper with each thrust. I could feel his balls rubbing against my cunt with each thrust. He grunted hard as he came, his legs shaking over me.

"That was fucking amazing," he said, "This is the most amazing New Years I've ever had." He gently pulled out, wrapping his arms around me from behind, kissing the back of my neck.

We cleaned up and nestled against each other on the couch. He poured us each a bit more champagne from a new bottle. "For the Gram?" he asked, sheepishly, holding

up his glass. We took a selfie, toasting each other for the

year to come, like every other couple that night.

Chapter 8: Squirting

Mr. A and I were wrapping up our first night vacationing in New Orleans. We were staying near the French Quarter on Toulouse Street in a very old apartment building. We had planned a three-day dom/sub sex vacation. We picked New Orleans as a city where anything goes. We figured we were less likely to be judged by anything anyone witnessed than anywhere else in the country. I had agreed to allow Mr. A to choose my attire each day. This is how I came to be wearing a pair of hot blank shorts that I argued were more like cheeky panties than shorts. He also had me in a sheer white top that barely covered by breast, which were adorned with circular nipple clamps with purple tassels dangling from each nipple. The outfit was finished off with a pair of black leather boots that came to my knees. At least they were comfortable. We had bar crawled half-way down Bourbon Street and were working our way back to the Airbnb.

"This is our last stop before heading home," Mr. A said as we sat down in a pair of leather chairs downstairs, away from most of the rowdy partiers. There was a long couch on the wall opposite us, but only a few people were downstairs. It was as private a spot as we had found all night. "I'm going to take some photos of you with my phone. Some could be embarrassing for you. Are you ready?" he asked.

"Yes, sir," I answered, feeling a bit tipsy from the last Hurricane I had sipped.

"Good. We'll start easy. Just simply sit and smile big. I want to capture how gorgeous that sheer top looks on you with those nipple clamps busting through." I had spent most of the night overly self-conscious about my skimpy outfit that would have gotten me arrested in any other city. I had received some odd looks, but more encouragement and compliments than anything. I had almost forgotten that my top was sheer until he reminded me.

"Perfect. Now lift your top up above your breasts, so I can get a better picture of you wearing those beautiful nipple clamps."

"Here?" I asked, looking around for anyone nearby paying attention. No one was.

"And here I thought you might avoid getting spanked tonight, but you just questioned an order. Let's try again. Lift up your shirt and turn towards me."

I faced him and blocked out any thoughts of people staring and quickly raised my shirt, waited for him to snap a few on his phone, then put it back down, taking a long drink of whiskey.

"See? Easy work. Next, stand up and put our hands on the table, butt popped out, then look back at me." I stood up and scanned the room again. This shot would definitely capture the crowd below us, but I doubted they could see me posing ridiculously. I quickly got into position and waited for him to take a few.

"These are hot," he said. "Last one. Pull those shorts halfway down your ass so that I can capture you plug." I turned my head and stared at him, eyes wide in disbelief. "That hesitation will cost you a longer spanking tonight," he said, shaking his head. I closed my eyes and pulled them down for maybe three seconds while he snapped a few. A quickly put them back on and sat back down, picking up my whiskey to drain it. He caught my arm.

"Relax, Sweetie. No one saw you, and if they did, they are currently jealous or hard right now, because that was hot. Sip your drink, don't knock it back. I need to lucid tonight." We finished our drinks and walked the last few blocks back to our weekend home. We were on the ninth floor which meant a scary elevator ride every time we left or returned to the apartment. The elevator was so old, I'm sure it was long past passing any codes to be deemed safe.

It was also slower that what we could walk had we been sober.

"Last step and be quick. Remove your shirt and shorts. I want you walking into our apartment in just your nipple clamps, butt plug, and boots."

"Um, no. I am not getting naked in this elevator," I argued back.

"Oh, okay. You are accepting an unpleasant punishment when we get inside the room?"
I put my head down, trying to decide. I was continuing to dig a rather large hole for myself. Our elevator was slowly making progress, closer to floor 9. I removed my top.

"Just my top," I said. He said nothing more, but smiled at me as I stood there, face and chest flushed from embarrassment. The elevator opened and I peered out, looking both ways to see if it was safe to walk the remaining 30 feet to our unit. The hallway was completely empty. Mr. A took his time finding our key card to let me in. As soon as he opened the door, I sprang through it. He laughed.

"I guess you don't like to be publicly naked," he said. "We'll try again tomorrow. But for now, you must be punished. I had planned some light and fun swats tonight, but this is forcing me to go harder. You need to learn to listen and respond without questioning. Do you agree?" he asked.

"Yes sir," I agreed, keeping my head bent down. I knew I was in trouble. He was pushing my boundaries tonight, but they were boundaries I had agreed to. I wasn't as brave or as bold as I imagined. The thought of my punishment filled me with trepidation. My head was feeling prickly, my ears hot from the anxiety. My cunt, on the other hand, was pulsating in response, already wet from the anticipation. He walked over to me, dropped to his knees and peeled my shorts to me knees. Immediately, the stabbed two fingers inside of me, hard and deep. I gasped in immediate pleasure. He removed them and put them in my mouth.

"Taste your pussy. It's already wet. You are in trouble. This part isn't for your pleasure. This is a lesson. If you cum during this punishment, you will not have any more orgasms this weekend. Are we clear on this?" he asked me in his sternest dom voice. I sucked his fingers, dutifully, tasting the muskiness that was all me, continued to suck until he removed his fingers. He bent down and removed my shorts around my boots, asking me to step out of them.

"Bend over the arm of the couch," he commanded. I knew he chose the arm of the couch because he knew I loved getting spanked over his knee. This was a punishment. He also knew the arm rest would rub against my cunt as he spanked me. I was hoping he'd keep the nipple clamps on so I couldn't feel my nipples harden against the rough couch fabric, but he remembered and roughly removed each clamp. My nipples were immediately rock hard and throbbing from the clamps. Each spink of the blades of the ceiling fan amplified the feeling.

"I am not going to tell you how many strikes you are getting. You will not be allowed to get up until I tell you to. I will not stop if you beg or cry. I will only stop if our secret word is used. Are we clear?" he asked. He really had me apprehensive about my punishment. I had never had to use my secret word before. Red Light. Such an unoriginal phrase. I had no doubts that he would stop immediately if I asked him. I was willing to be punished. I was not mentally prepared. He popped my ass with a paddle that I didn't even know he had. I let out a loud gasp as the first strike. He quickly popped my other ass cheek, and this time I sucked in as much air as possible while tightening both ass cheeks.

"Relax your ass. You know better," he said as more blows reigned down. The pain was intense as I couldn't keep up with the internalizing one blow before another struck. He covered both ass cheeks quickly, not pausing until every inch was covered with a mark. My legs writhed and wiggled during the last few blows. I was trying any way to endure, crying out from the pain. He stopped and put down the paddle. I heard him pour himself a drink. He didn't speak to me as he sipped his glass. I could feel welts rising in many places along my tender cheeks. They were emanating heat that contrasted with the coolness of the fan. The after-effects were exquisite. I felt my cunt drip from arousal, squeezed tight against the arm of the couch. My clit immediately responded to this with a deep pulsing. I was so ready to erupt. I wanted to grab my nipples and fuck the arm rest, to utilize the heat's effects before it was only pain from the blows.

"Round two," he said. "I will be using my hand this time. Are you starting to understand what a brat you were this evening?"

"Yes, sir. I'm sorry," I said, sounding like a spoiled child.

"I doubt you are sorry, but I appreciate the apology." Remember, no moving until you are instructed to move. I gasped and yelled out as I felt cold burning liquid trickle down my right cheek, then my left. He was dribbling his whiskey only my welts, causing the burning to light back up before he laid one hand on me. Setting his glass down, he wasted no time striking. My ass was wet from the whiskey, amplifying each strike. I cried out with each blow, repeating "I'm sorry. I won't be bratty anymore" to him as he ignored my pleas. I wasn't sure how I was going to sit down tomorrow. He stopped abruptly and pulled out the butt plug that I had been wearing for several hours. He shoved it in my mouth, plugging my cries and continued several more strikes. This time he focused on the area just below my ass, tender skin that never feels the paddle. Without the ability to cry out, tears ran down my face. He stopped. I didn't move, was willing to do anything he asked of me.

I heard him fixing another drink. He walked back over and moved a kitchen chair near me, sitting in it. He reached around and pulled the plug from my mouth.

"Turn around and suck me," he ordered. I moved from the arm of the couch and knelt in front of him. He had removed his pants. His cock was fully erect and twitching to be swallowed. I didn't waste any time. I wanted him to know how sorry I was for my misbehavior. I took him long and deep, mixing strokes with my hands. I bent lower to work all around his balls, but he stopped me. "Just stick to my cock. Suck it rhythmically and hard. Be a whore, not a lover, he ordered." I did as instructed, sucking without playing but fucking him hard with my mouth. He pressed his hand gently behind my head, guiding my mouth lower and lower over his cock. I gagged, but he did not release me. I took him deeper, sucked harder. "Are you ready to obey me?" he asked. I nodded. "Good. You are not done being punished yet, but that is a start. I ordered fresh baked cookies to be delivered while you were soaking in the paddle beating. When it comes, you will answer the door and sign the bill for the cookies, dressed as you are now. I'll put the clamps back on and the plug back in –just as you should have been dressed in the elevator. First, finish sucking me off. If the driver gets here before your finished, they are going to see your gaping asshole, stretched from the plug.

I hated him just a little for this but knew I was obliged to participate. I dreaded the look on the driver's face as I opened the door. I couldn't imagine what my ass looked like, but I knew it was the harshest spanking he had ever delivered to me. Ignoring all these thoughts, I went down on him with what I imagined to be a whore's

expertise, completely focusing on this one job. He pulled

out right at the point of climax and pumped semen all over

my face and chest. I was bathed in his mess. He smiled,

approvingly.

"Don't wipe off. It's a bonus for the driver, he said,

kissing me on the head– his first act of kindness since we

entered the apartment. "Sit back on the couch and relax. I'll

get you a drink." He fixed us each a drink and I nervously

chatted with him while waiting for the delivery. I was

hoping the cum dried before anyone answered the door. I

didn't know if I wanted the person to be male or female,

old or young. I wanted to run and hide in the bedroom. The

knock on the door was loud. Definitely male, I thought. He

raised his eyebrows at me with a big smile. "This is so

much better than the elevator," he said, getting his phone

ready to capture the moment. I opened the door to see a

younger male staring down at me. He was probably in his

early 20s. He smiled and immediately dropped his eyes low, handing me the small box. I grabbed them, used the box to sign the receipt and quickly shut the door. I didn't breathe during the 30 second transaction.

"Wow. Amazingly hot, sweetie. That dude is probably going to jerk off in his car before he goes back to the store. So hot. I'm already hard again," he said, leading me to the bedroom. "I think we have unfinished business."

He laid me on the bed and kissed me long and hard, his tongue pushing deep into my mouth, hungry for more. He removed the clamps and smothered his mouth over each breast, continuing his aggressiveness by biting my nipples to the point of almost pain with incredible pleasure. My cunt ached for his touch. I thought I might explode with the lightest touch of anything on it. He spread my legs and slid inside me, pumping hard and fast.

"Fuck, you are sopping wet," he said, maneuvering my legs around his neck, driving his cock deeper inside me.

He reached around and found a pillow to prop under my ass then pulled me higher toward the ceiling, exposing me ass.

"Remove the plug," he instructed, "I'm going to ass fuck you as hard as I was paddling you moments ago." I pulled out the plug and immediately felt his cock out of my vagina and in my ass, slipping in fully from the gape created from the plug. The position created an angle that allowed his cock to drive deeper into my ass, slamming hard each time. He had his arms wrapped around my legs for support as he pulled me hard and deep. I fondled my nipples, pinching each with the same intensity. His cocked jabbed deep and connected with my G-spot, thrusting quickly, over and over. I felt myself spraying all over us.

"I'm squirting! I'm squirting!" I exclaimed, completely surprising us both. The spray intensified his desire, and he shuddered into me as he came. I dropped my legs down and gently pushed his head towards the mess between my legs. He obeyed. I kept massaging and pinching my nipples as he licked up my fluids, treated my cunt as dessert. As soon as his tongue brushed over my clit, I erupted as well, pushing his head down harder and bucking against him, my legs so tight around him, I thought I might be suffocating him, but I kept up the pressure, screaming out as all the pent-up desire from the entirety of the evening crashed over me and through my cunt. I let everything go, felt the pleasure through every nerve ending.

"This bed is soaked from all of us," I said. "Where are we going to sleep tonight?"

"You soaked the sheets," he said, smiling. "Maybe you need to be punished for that," he teased, rubbing my ass tenderly.

Chapter 9: Pull-ups

Mr. A and I were having a play week. During play weeks, I am completely submissive to him when in the house. If either of us needed a time out from playing, it was agreed upon, and then we'd resume our roles. He knew my boundaries and loved pushing them. Pee play was one of those areas that we disagreed about, mostly that it wasn't my favorite thing. So, he used it sparingly. But on this morning, I knew upon waking that it was going to be a long day.

I always slept naked, and typically peed as soon as I woke up. On this Saturday, Mr. A stopped me as soon as I started to rise. "Hold on," he said, raising himself. He went to the linen closet and pulled out an unopened batch of adult pull-ups. My eyes grew big as I was imagining his plan for the day.

"You will be wearing pull-ups all day today, so please put one on now," he said as he opened the bag.

"But I already have to pee," I protested.

"I know," he smiled. "So, put the pull-up on and pee in the pull-up." I put it on but continued to protest. It felt horrible. The rough material scratched against my crotch. I felt ridiculous. To make it worse, he threw me a pair of leggings to put over them.

"I won't be able to pee in the pull-up," I argued. "I haven't peed myself since I was five."

He just shrugged and gave his orders. "When you must pee, you will go in the pull-up, then you will tell me that you've wet your pants. I will change you, but you will be punished. This will be our day today," he said, then warned, "And you will drink a normal amount of fluids."

I held it in as I brushed my teeth and went downstairs, thinking about avoiding morning coffee, but Mr. A went straight for the pot and made enough for us both, expecting me to drink. By the end of the cup, I was

squeezing with everything I had to not pee myself. Mr. A

was smiling but continued to drink his coffee. Then he

sprang up and fetched the dog's leash.

"Come on," he said, "The pup needs to go out and

pee as well."

"I'll stay here," I said, but he protested.

"Nope. You will walk with us or suffer bigger

consequences when I return," he threatened. I slipped into

my flip-flops and headed out the door. I didn't make it very

far. He was walking fast, and I couldn't squeeze my legs

together enough at that pace. It started to involuntarily

trickle out of me.

"Stop," I said, and leaned my back against a tree,

just a few blocks from our house. I relaxed and the urine

flowed from me. I felt the pull-up fill up with my liquid, its

warmth flooding me. I was shocked that my leggings were

staying dry. Mr. A watched in fascination and amusement

as I let it flow. Finished, I started making strides towards the house.

"No," he said, "We always walk the pup a mile in the morning. You'll will have to wait for me to change you when we get home." The walk was miserable as every step felt like I had an oversized pad between my legs. I was sure every neighbor that was also out walking knew I had peed myself, could somehow smell me. Finally, we made it home, but the day's humiliation was only beginning. Mr. A took me to the spare bedroom where he had laid out a makeshift changing station. He sat on the bed and said, "Stand in front me so that I can get you out of the wet diaper." I moved in front of him, and he pulled down my leggings first, working them off my feet. Then he pulled the pull up down, and I stepped out of it. He caressed his hand over my front side, then my butt cheeks.

"You are a little wet from pee," he said. "You were a bad girl for peeing your pants outside. Bend over my knee, please, before I clean you up."

I knew not to protest and bent over to accept my spanking. He made sure I knew I had been bad with each smack, but it was over quickly.

"Now, lay back so that I can clean you off," he instructed.

I moved on my back with my legs bent. He took a wet wipe from a container he had laid out and gently wiped my front side then motioned my legs up to swipe around my back side. He already had the pull ups in the room and worked another one up my legs and around my cunt and butt again. He helped me up and handed me the leggings again. I went about my day cleaning and doing normal Saturday chores. I tried to abstain from drinking water, but he kept shoving my water bottle in front of me, instructing me to drink. The second time I had to pee, I was willing to get it over with faster.

"I have to go again," I said.

"Already? I figured you'd be able to hold it in a few more hours. I'm genuinely surprised," he said.

"Nope. Ready to go now," I answered back.

"Okay. Well, let's get you back to the spare bedroom." He held my hand as he led me back to the room but tapped my head to get on my knees as we entered.

"You want me to pee on my knees?" I asked.

"Yes," he said. "I want you to pee while sucking my dick. I'm going to give you two minutes. If you don't pee while sucking me, you will get spanked and then we will start over again. Now, on your knees, please," he said as he started unbuckling his belt. "The timer starts now," he said.

I started sucking on him in a very traditional way, finding it hard to concentrate on a blow job and on peeing at the same time. I kept his cock in my mouth but couldn't force out any pee, even though I really had to go.

"Time," he announced, "Get up and touch your toes." I stood up and bent over. He yanked my pullup down just enough to expose my ass. With one hand over my crotch. He smacked the middle of my ass five times, hard, before pulling my pull up back on and commanding, "back on your knees." I knew his timer was already ticking down. We repeated this pattern three more times before I finally relaxed my mouth over his cock and allowed him to be in control of the thrusting as I closed my eyes and focused on peeing. I let out a small moan as I felt the sweet release into the pull-up. Mr. A started thrusting harder as he read my face. He pulled out and came all over my face as I was pulsing the last drops out of me.

"Back on the bed," he said, with a small smile, the routine already familiar. He wiped my backside first with some roughness as each red mark was on fire, reminded me of how long it took me, then moved to my front. He took my hand and moved it to my nipples, my cue to play with them while he cleaned me up. I swirled them around, squeezing each with pleasure as he watched. He started circling the wet wipe around my clit, fingering me with his free hand. My hips rose to meet his fingers, my fingers squeezing each nipple harder as my cunt swelled around his fingers. He kept the wet wipe on my clit, kept using circular motions to rub until my body gave in to the sensation as I cried out in pleasure.

He waited until my breathing returned to normal before removing the wet wipe and reaching for a new pull up.

"This is probably going to sting a bit on your sore bottom," he said, shrugging his shoulders in a half-hearted apology.

I helped him slide the pull-up up, and replied, "I'll live. Just maybe use another wipe to clean the cum off my face?" I asked.

"Oh Baby, you misread me again," he said. "It won't be time to wash your face until bedtime. Maybe you should try harder to stay clean." It was going to be a very long day. I sighed to myself but also felt completely satisfied.

Chapter 2: Peeing during the Act

Thursday, 3:00 PM. I sat at my desk, finishing up mindless paperwork, ready for it to be 4:00 PM when I could head home. Thursday nights were designated play dates for Mr. A and me. What we did varied from week to week. I left Mr. A in charge of these nights, trusting he would have something fun and kinky in mind. A text came through my phone, and I glanced over. I instantly went wet as I saw who it was from. I opened it, looking around casually to see if anyone was nearby. *Please begin holding your pee* was all it said. Mild alarm shot through me. I sip water all day long and hadn't been to the restroom since lunch. I usually went just before I left work. Should I go right now? He wouldn't know. Taking a deep breath, I decided to obey. I wasn't sure what he had in mind, but I knew my anxiety over needing to pee would be beneficial to our session later.

I was greeted with a glass of wine as I walked through the door. "Thanks," I said, taking a sip. "I guess we are starting early tonight," I inquired.

"I'm very excited," he grinned. "And I assumed you were already ready to pee, so I wanted to start with the water sports, if that's okay."

"Sure," I agreed. "What are we going to be doing? I very much have to pee."

"Holding. I want you to hold your pee until you feel like you can't hold it anymore. Then you are going to fuck me and hopefully pee while I am inside you."

"We can certainly try," I said, taking a bigger drink of my wine.

"Great! if you want to head to the basement, I have an outfit laid out for you in the spare bedroom. I thought it might feel better to hang out down there where there is less lighting."

We had converted our basement to an Airbnb space. We had two rooms that were connected with a small bathroom in between. We had ceramic tile installed throughout both rooms. The bedroom was simple. It only held a queen-sized bed and a dresser. But we covered the mattress with a waterproof covering to protect the mattress from any spills or accidents when we had clients occupying the space. It also gave us a great space to experiment with water sports. The connecting room was a second living room. It contained an L shaped leather sectional that was very comfortable and easy to clean. We had a mini bar downstairs as well, equipped with a cart of bourbons and red wines.

I walked into the bedroom and found a black lace teddy on the bed with a butt plug. It was a small glass plug–just big enough to press against my bladder and create a bigger feeling of fullness. I stripped out of my work clothes and slipped the plug in first. It immediately stimulated my entire lower region. I squeezed against it and tugged at my nipples, aching for Mr. A's touch already. I stepped into the teddy, if that was even the correct term. It was not much of anything. It had cutouts for each breast. It was crotchless, but there was a thin piece of fabric on the backside that kept the whole thing from falling off. Other than that, I was fully exposed. I assessed myself in the full-length mirror attached to the door and nodded in approval. The outfit was hot. I walked into the basement living room with confidence. Mr. A took his time drinking me in, his eyes filled with approval. I straddled his lap and pulled him in for a kiss. His hands automatically went to my nipples, and I moaned my approval. The pressure from my bladder, combined with the butt plug was causing a throbbing in my entire groin region screaming for attention. I was really hoping we'd get right to the action.

"How about one more drink, before we get to the sex?" he suggested.

"I don't know if I can get down another drink without peeing all over this room," I said.

"Well, if you think you are so ready to piss your pants than you can pee while fucking me. Let's do it," he said. "But each time you fail, I am going to spank you, and then we will sit for a drink."

"Deal," I said, headed to the bed. "I am ready to burst."

He left our drinks in the living room and followed me into the bedroom. I stripped the covers back and crawled in bed. Mr. A dropped his pants and motioned me towards him. "'Suck me," he ordered. I laid on my stomach and swallowed his semi-hard cock, working it with purpose. It grew very quickly in my mouth. I wrapped my hands around his ass, directing him deeper inside my mouth as I teased my rhythm and intensity. He stroked my hair with one hand and played with a nipple with his other hand. The ache in my groin was so intense, I was ready to explode.

"Fuck me, please," I said, anxious to feel relief. He climbed in bed and motioned for me to straddle him. He slid into me easily, my readiness apparent by the wetness dripping between my legs. I rode his cock slowly, taking all of him and enjoying the fullness from the plug.

"You have one minute to piss with me inside you," he said softly, starting the timer on his watch. I shifted my focus to relieving my bladder. I squeezed but nothing happened. I grinded all around the base of his cock then squeezed again. Still nothing. I felt so full inside, but the piss would not flow. I closed my eyes and concentrated while Mr. A played with both nipples, tugging and pulling at them. The timer beeped. He reached into the bedside table and retrieved two nipple clamps. Without saying a word, he placed a clamp on each nipple, tightening just enough for my nipples to lightly burn.

"Flip over and across my lap," he ordered. A moved across his lap, hoping I didn't pee on him while being punished. I immediately felt even more pressure from laying on my stomach. He was quick. He applied five hard slaps with his hand to my right butt cheek and then five hard slaps to my left butt cheek. I tensed up immediately, clamping with every muscle I had to not pee. "Head back into the living room and pour us drinks, please," he instructed, giving me a light swat as I walked away.

I couldn't imagine any more liquid entering my bladder, but I picked up my glass of wine, poured him more whiskey, and sat back down on the couch, my cheeks a bit tender from the minor punishment. The nipple clamps were screaming back to me as their weight was tugging at them, exacerbating the intense need I felt to release my body. Mr. A sat beside me with a smile on his face, raising his glass towards mine. He knew I wasn't ready the first time, let me try, knowing I'd fail. "I really thought I'd be able to pee," I said, reading his thoughts and smiling sheepishly.

"Oh, I know you thought that," he said nodding, "I also knew you wouldn't. So, enjoy the wine. I'm in no hurry. We can try again in a few minutes. Just one last thing, he said. Please finger fuck yourself while sipping your wine," he ordered with a devilish grin, clearly loving this game. I kept the wine in my right hand and sank two fingers inside me, feeling my slick walls. I moved them slowly back and forth, focusing on not getting too excited. I'd be punished more if I came before it was time. "Drink," he reminded me. I took a long drink of the wine and bucked up towards my fingers. "Would you rather piss with your fingers inside of you?" he asked. "I'd love to watch you."

That idea was even more horrifying. "No," I replied, "I don't think I'd be able to pee on my back. But I think I can do it with you inside me this time. I'm ready to try again."

He raised an eyebrow, but said, "Lead the way."

I drank another long swig of the wine and made my way to the bed again. He got back into position on his back, and I knew to begin with my face between his legs. I suckled his cock until it was standing fully erect. I stroked it with my mouth, back and forth several times before straddling him again. He rubbed the back of his hand over the small tip of my nipples protruding from the clamps. I thought I might cum without any other stimulation. I kept my legs bent, sitting on my feet, in more of a position I'd be in if I were to pee in the toilet. I sat down on him slowly, bringing him fully into my cunt before rising again and almost pulling out before dropping back down again. He let out a soft moan.

"Starting the timer," he warned in a husky voice. I settled down on his cock and went completely still. Eyes still closed, I took a deep breath and focused on relaxing completely rather than flexing my inner muscles. I felt a small buildup of urine attempt to work its way out. At first, the fullness of the plug and his cock was too much. It felt like it was trapped inside. But then more release came, and a flow started. Mr. A started pumping against me, noticeably excited that pee was now flowing everywhere. An entire day's worth worked its way out of me. I remained motionless, totally taken by the feeling of relieving myself with a cock inside me. The backside of my legs were soaked with pee. I could feel the wetness spreading all over the bed. Mr. A was bucking and pumping hard against me, squeezing my breasts against the nipple clamps. He slowed his fucking as my urine stream slowed. When I was completely relieved, he held his cock still and pulled me in for a sensual kiss.

"That was so hot, babe," he said, releasing the clamps. "Please sit on my face." I pulled myself from his cock and worked my way forward, not caring about how soaked the sheets were, fully aware that my cunt, ass, and legs were covered in urine. I held onto the headboard and presented my lips to him, as he applied pressure to each nipple. The sensitive sensation, part pain from the release of the clamps, and part sheer pleasure from his hands working them, intensified the nerve endings around my clitoris. It throbbed to be touched. I thrust my hips forward as he clamped down, eating me as if I were an exotic delicacy, savoring each flavor. As soon as he grazed the nub of my clit, I screamed out in ecstasy. I froze my body as I let him feast. I continued to scream, feeling on the edge of not being able to take the pleasure, but needing the release with every fiber inside of me. I stayed frozen for what seemed an eternity. Eventually, my breathing slowed, and my screaming became lower moans of pleasure. Mr. A. released his grip, and I moved back down.

"On your knees," he said, desire spilling from those words. I had almost forgotten he hadn't unloaded yet, took in his fully erect cock with my eyes. He removed my plug and spread my ass cheeks before plunging his tongue in, his fingers finding my cunt, swollen from my orgasm, but still very stimulated. He guided his cock into my ass, the plug having created an easy entry. I lowered my tits to the wet sheets, hiking my butt higher into the air for him. He fucked my ass with quick hard strokes, ramming the full force of his cock into me each time. It didn't take long before he let out several loud groans of satisfaction, filling my ass with his fluids. He rested behind me a few moments, regaining his breathing and stroking my ass lovingly. I slid off the bed and headed immediately to the shower, feeling thoroughly satiated and relaxed. When I came out of the shower, Mr. A was cleaning up our mess.

"Should we go out to dinner?" he asked. "I really don't feel like making more messes tonight." I smiled and nodded in agreement.

Chapter 10: Job Interview

Mr. A and I set aside special time at least one weekend a month that is dedicated to more in-depth play with each other. We often incorporate role-playing into our sex fantasies. One recurring role is that of secretary and boss. The following story reflects a role-played job interview.

Every day I make it a habit of searching job openings to see if there is anything available that trumps my current position. I finally found an ad that caught my eye. *Submissive office assistant wanted for small office. Job duties include light typing, filing, and pleasing the boss in any way asked. Must be willing to submit and be okay with spanking, anal play, and water sports. To apply, please send a full body picture in a swimsuit or lingerie along with a short bio of qualifications.*

This was definitely the type of dream job I had always imagined for myself. I set up my tripod, slipped on by favorite lingerie ensemble, and constructed an email

reply:

Dr Sir: I am writing to apply for the office assistant position available for your company. I have experience with typing and filing and make very few errors. I pay great attention to detail. I am an excellent sub for this reason. I am always eager to please and do what I am told. I have been spanked numerous times and have experienced with anal play. I do not have experience with water sports, but I am willing and eager to learn. Please consider me for an interview for this position. Thank you.

I checked my emails obsessively for the next few days and finally received a response the following Friday:

Ms G, I recently received your job inquiry for a submissive office assistant. I would like to set up an interview for this position. Please come to my office tomorrow evening at 6:00 PM. The dress code for the evening includes a white button-down dress shirt that is sheer. Please be braless. Please wear gray dress pants with at least 3-inch heels. I expect you to be groomed and in top form. I look forward to meeting you.

I searched my closet for the proper attire and found exactly what Sir was asking for. I also had a variety of high heels so was able to piece together the perfect interview outfit. I quickly scheduled a spa day for Saturday morning that included a full Brazilian wax with the butt strip included, manicure, pedicure, and hair styling. The women at the spa thought I was preparing for a hot date. They had

no idea I was preparing to reveal all at a job interview.

I arrived at Sir's office at exactly 6:00 pm.

However, I had removed my shoes while driving as the

high heels made it difficult to control the pedals. I put my

heels back on and freshened up my lipstick with a quick

assessment in my car mirror. I knocked on his door at 6:05

pm.

When Sir answered the door, I was taken back by

his sex appeal. Standing several inches above me, he wore

a dark tailored suit and tie. The pants were just snug

enough for me to make out the outline of his cock, and a

blushed a bit, already aroused by him. He did not seem as

impressed with me. He answered the door expressionless

and led me to his office, located in his basement. He had a

large space that included a desk for himself, and a small

table set up for an office assistant. I noticed a single chaise

lounge in one corner and a television suspended from the

ceiling. He did not offer me a place to sit. He sat behind his desk and offered his hand which I promptly shook.

"Ms G, I presume?" he asked. "You were five minutes late."

"Sorry, I pulled up to your place at 6:00. It just took me a few minutes to get out of the car and to your door."

"Do you regularly make it a habit of showing up to work five minutes late? When I asked you to be here at 6:00, I assumed you would be knocking on my door by 6:00, maybe even a few minutes early, but certainly not five minutes late." He seemed genuinely annoyed that I was a few minutes late. The annoyance in his voice caused a slight pitch change in his voice that I found strangely attractive.

"Completely my fault, Sir. I apologize," I said, nervous that I had already messed up this interview.

"This interview might as well start a bit non-traditionally as you have already broken a rule. As my office assistant, when and if you break a rule or make a

mistake, I will correct you immediately. We can let this be

a trial run. Please bend over the desk and prepare to be

disciplined," Sir said, now with more of an amused tone

even though he was trying to be in the role of a serious

disciplinarian.

I stared at him for a moment in disbelief. I knew

this was a position for a submissive, but I wasn't mentally

prepared to complete any submissive acts during the

interview. I reluctantly complied, feeling immediately like

the girl from The Secretary movie as I put my forearms on

his desk and bent over. With my head turned to face the

wall, I saw him remove a paddle from the wall. It appeared

to be a college fraternity paddle that was hung to show his

university and fraternity associations. He brought the

paddle over and said, "Since this is your first infraction and

our first time meeting, I will go easy this session. Your

pants may remain up. I am going to deliver 10 whacks for

your lateness. In the future, if there is a future, please be prompt. When you are receiving discipline, you are not to cry out, protest, or plead for less. Is that clear?"

I felt myself grow warm in my groin as he spoke to me so sternly. I couldn't help getting excited while also feeling like I had already ruined the interview.

"Yes, Sir," I replied, hoping I'd be able to redeem myself. He swung harder than I had anticipated, the paddle meeting both ass cheeks. I involuntarily hopped a bit in response.

"Stand still," he commanded as another whack reigned across my butt, this one even harder. I flinched but remained still. By the third hit, I felt my groin grow moist. But my ass was stinging beneath my clothes. I wanted to feel his hands caressing them. The next blows were steady and remained hard. He did not speak until all 10 had been delivered.

"Stand up," he said as he replaced the paddle on the wall. "You mentioned in your interview that you have typing skills. Is that correct?" I nodded, not trusting my voice. "Great. Do you have experience with dictation? I like to dictate while my office assistant types what I am speaking. If you are ready, I'd like to try this out and see how you do."

"Sure," I said. "I am a fast typist but have not typed dictation before, so that is new to me."

"Sit at the table with the laptop on it. You will find it already on a Word document. Open it and get your hand situated on the keys, please." I walked over to the table and sat on the hard chair as softly as possible, my ass stinging from the whacks. I opened the laptop and the screen lip up to a blank word document. I placed my hands on the keyboard and looked up at Sir. He began his dictation as I did my best to keep up: *A slutty girl is sitting in front of me.*

I can see her hard nipples through her shirt. I am fairly

certain the spanking I gave her turned her on.

He stopped dictating, and I looked up. "Read back to me what you typed," he instructed, the smirk on his face returning.

"A slutty girl is sitting in front of me. I can see her hard nipples through her shirt. I am fairly certain the spanking I gave her turned her on," I said, trying to keep my voice steady and not taking anything personally.

"Perfect," he said. "Now get up and bend over the desk again. I'm going to read over your work."

I bent over again, wondering if I was going to get more whacks from typing too slow or for something else. Instead, he glanced at the document and said, "It looks good. We are ready to move on. As I stated in the job description, you must be agreeable to many sexual encounters at my command. If you are still agreeable, I'd like to move to a lower body inspection. Just nod if you agree."

I nodded, remaining bent over his desk. "Very good," he said, "Now reach down and unbutton and unzip your pants so that I can pull them down."

I kept one forearm on the table and used the other to unclasp my pants. He moved close enough to me that I could feel him breathing behind me, but he did not speak as he pulled my dress pants and panties down to my ankles. He lightly stroked my tender ass, and I gasped lightly, not expecting such a tender caress. He moved his hand against my thigh, indicating he wanted my legs spread further, and I complied. Next, he placed his index finger in my cunt, barely felt due to the wetness swimming inside me.

"Very wet, I see." he said, "I love it." He removed his finger from my cunt and placed it in my ass, working it back and forth. "Nice and tight. The interview is headed in a very positive direction," he continued. He walked around his desk and opened his top desk drawer and pulled out a stainless-steel butt plug with a hot pink jewel that protruded out slightly. It was bigger than most plugs I had encountered, and I squirmed a bit, knowing that was going in my ass.

"Don't worry. I have lube," he said, removing a tube from his drawer as well. He walked back to my backside and lathered my ass with lube, this time inserting two fingers. I gasped louder than expected, feeling the sensual sensation erupt through my body. My nipples grew harder, rubbing against the rough fabric of my shirt. "Tell me you love this," he commanded.

"I love this," I repeated back to him quietly, a bit reluctant to repeat him.

"Always address me as sir. Say it again," he prompted.

"I love this, Sir," I said again, trying to sound more confident.

"Good. Stay relaxed and spread your butt cheeks so that I can insert this plug. You will wear it for the remainder of the interview."

I placed my tits on his cold desk and spread my ass cheeks, feeling their warmth from the spanking, imagining them red and angry looking. He pressed the plug against my ass, working it into my tight opening. I felt my body resisting it and took in a deep breathing trying to relax. He pushed with gentle but firm force and my ass accepted it. For just a moment, I felt a burning sensation around the rim of my asshole, followed by an erotic sensation of fullness. The weight of the plug caused my lips and folds to begin swelling with arousal. He stood up and faced me again.

"I didn't mention oral sex, but I assume you are fine sucking my cock?" he asked.

"Yes Sir," I said back, remembering my manners.

"Great. I need an assistant that likes to suck cock. Let's see how you do," he said, unzipping his pants and pulling out his cock, fully erect. He sat in his chair and said, "Pull your pants up and get on your knees under my desk. I want you to suck me while I read through my emails." I stood up and pulled my pants up, trying to discreetly pinch my ass to get the plug in a somewhat comfortable position. I bent down between Sir's legs and stroked his beautiful cock with my hands first before placing my mouth over his head, savoring the smooth texture before exploring his shaft with my lips. I worked my mouth up and down several times, hoping he was enjoying my work. Only when I suckled his balls did he let out the slightest moan. I began to feel better about my job chances. I continued to tease his cock while he read his emails. Still fully erect, he cut me off.

"That's enough for now," he said. "Get up and on your feet. We are moving into the bathroom for this last part." He opened a door and led me into his bathroom. It contained a bath/shower combo, small sink, and toilet.

There was a drain in the middle of the tiled floor. One wall included a floor to ceiling mirror. "I need to see how you respond to water sports. You mentioned not having any experience, so this could be challenging. Here is what is going to happen. You will piss your pants. Once you do, I will piss all over your frontside. You will stand there and take it as I cover you with my piss," he said.

I wasn't sure how to respond. This was far-reaching for me, but I had agreed, and I did want his cock inside me. I was willing to do almost anything to feel his body all over me. "Okay," I said, very quietly.

"Okay," he repeated. "I hope you came hydrated. If not, I have shots of whiskey you can do."

"I might need the whiskey shots," I said, relieved to be stalling for a few minutes. He left and came back with a bottle of whiskey and two shot glasses. He poured one for each of us and handed one to me.

"Cheers," he said, smiling at me, clearly enjoying my nervousness. We tipped our glasses to each other and shot them back. He poured water for me from the bathroom tap, and I drank a cup of it as well. I stood there for what seemed an eternity, willing urine to begin. I had never as an adult peed my pants. I wasn't sure I'd be able to do it, but I was desperate for this job. Sir stood patiently waiting. Finally, he said, "Another shot?" I handed him my glass. We each threw back another, and I followed mine with another cup of water. I was starting to feel the warmness of the whiskey. Very unexpectedly, Sir moved towards me and wrapped his fingers in my hair, then drew me in for an unexpected kiss. He pressed his tongue inside my mouth, finding my own tongue, and I kissed him back with all the longing I felt in my groin, a smile growing on my face. I was desperate to win him over. He stood back a few steps and smiled at me, hands on his hips, playfully waiting for me to piss myself.

"Is it okay if I ran some water in the sink?" I asked, thinking the sound of water might help.

"Whatever it takes," he said, smiling bigger. I turned on the cold tap and walked back to my spot, closing my eyes and willing myself to focus on the sound of the water and will my brain to believe I was sitting on a toilet. And just like that, I felt my urine stream flowing. I kept my eyes closed, so embarrassed I was doing this in front of someone, until Sir ordered, "Open your eyes." I opened them and caught myself in the mirror. The urine was darkening my grey pants on both sides. A puddle was developing on the floor. I could feel wetness all over my legs and feet. I stood frozen to my spot. I willed myself to look at Sir, the embarrassment and humiliation on my face unmistakable. He had dropped his pants and held his erect cock in his hand, which was the one sign of approval I needed.

"Don't move," he ordered. "Keep those pretty eyes open and looking at me," he said, as he steadied his cock towards me and aimed at my chest. I had little time to register in my mind that he intended to piss on me. I stood frozen, trying to reconcile the idea. He did not hesitate but began pissing at the center of my chest, spraying me with his fluid. He worked to soak all my shirt, my neck, and more of my pants. I gasped at the shock of being soaked in a combination of our fluids. I glanced in the mirror and saw the effect. My breasts and nipples were fully visible through my piss-soaked shirt that now clung to my body. My pants were now a darker shade of gray. They also clung to my legs. He stared at me for a long three seconds before pulling me in for a long, hungry kiss, not flinching from any of the wetness that transferred from me to him. He inhaled deeply, approving of the smell our scents created.

"Strip and bend over the sink," he instructed, as he began removing his clothes. I was a mess of emotion. I felt completely embarrassed with our piss all over the place, but at the same time, was fully aroused. Sir sensed my confusion and took a moment to caress my backside, lightly wet from the urine. I let out a small sigh of pleasure, relieved he wanted to touch me. With the plug still in, he guided his cock in my dripping cunt. He moved his cock in and out slowly, hitting the deepest area of my cunt. I gasped as he grabbed a nipple and tugged harshly. I expected him to cum in seconds. Instead, he paused and keeping his cock inside me, pulled out the plug. "I'm going to put my cock in your ass if that is okay with you," he whispered in my ear. I nodded, not able to speak. I felt him gently pull out of my cunt and dircct himself to my ass. Without being instructed, I pulled my ass cheeks back for him. The plug created the perfect entry, and it slipped in like a glove created just for me. Firmly inside me, he reached in his medicine cabinet and produced a clit sucker, turned it on, and handed it to me without further instruction. I placed it over my clit as he pressed down on one of my nipples. The combination of the fullness of his cock in my ass with the suckling vibration of the sex toy caused me to scream out in pleasure. Ripples of relief ran through me as I came hard against the sink. I squeezed together as my orgasm continued, and he rammed his cock deeper inside my ass, filling me with his erection. As I began to relax my groin, he started pumping harder and faster, working my hips towards him with each thrust. I could feel his ball sack press against my lips with each thrust. I thought I might erupt again as my swelling intensified every nerve he was hitting. He let out a series of groans as he stiffened behind me. It felt like his cock and balls were deep inside me, almost as if I was partially wearing him. I wanted us to exist stuck in this moment. Eventually, he pulled out and turned me around, kissing me with a gentleness that expressed his approval of our connection.

"You may rinse first," he said, pulling away and pointing me towards the shower while pulling on a robe that was hanging from the door. "I can start filling out paperwork for a new hire if you are agreeable to the position?" he asked almost shyly.

"Yes Sir," I said, smiling up at him as I started the water, just a bit sad to wash away all that we had just created.

Chapter 11: An evening of submission

We recently had our backyard transformed into an inviting area to entertain friends, Airbnb clients, or to entertain each other. We extended our privacy fence and planted enough greenery to have certain areas completely private from our neighbors. The area includes a salt-water hot tub, outdoor shower and firepit. It's easily accessible from our basement doors and a short walk lit by solar lights embedded close to the ground. We were in that sweet spot of weather where the days were still warm, but the evenings cool enough to welcome a fire and a hot tub soak. Mr. A had asked me to clear my Saturday evening schedule for some outdoor playtime. Our busy schedules had prevented any recent play, and we were both ready to go full throttle. I gave him permission to plan out our evening to whatever he desired. I would submit. Mr. A knew my boundaries, and I knew he would push them. I was ready for it: an entirely submissive evening.

We moved through the day with our normal weekend routine. He spent a great deal of the day in his office, while I did the mundane chores required on the weekends such as grocery shopping and catching up the laundry. At 5:00 I was in the shower getting ready for Mr. A to have his way with me. I prepped myself by carefully shaving every bit of hair growing from my groin down, replaying past play sessions in my head, and surprising myself with the level of arousal brought by simply thinking about what we create together. I used a cane sugar body scrub that left my skin completely invigorated, my nipples fully erect and yearning to be suckled. I grazed over them with the loofah sponge, and gave in to their achiness, dropped the sponge and grabbed each nipple, squeezing them with my thumbs and fingers. I picked the loofah sponge back up and inserted the long wooden handle in my cunt, working it in and out as my wetness lubricated it. My fingers found my clit, the first light touch sending a light shock through my body. My eyes remained closed as I focused on the image of Mr. A's hands all over my body. Just as suddenly as I started, I stopped abruptly, hearing Mr. A cough lightly.

"Well, I can see your evening is starting off nicely," he said, watching me from a distance, our walk-in shower revealing my self-play. "Please continue," he said, "but don't cum. That would require more punishment than I had planned for tonight." With an audience, my shower play changed slightly. I felt the redness that spread over my chest from the embarrassment of getting caught. My cunt told a different story as it throbbed with fullness. It begged me to finish what I had started. I went back to caressing my nipples and fucking myself with the sponge handle, but used a lighter pull on my nipple and stayed clear of my clit.

"Oh sweetie, what I saw earlier was more aggressive. Don't hold back now. Play with your clit. Just exercise control," he said, smiling as he took a sip of his whiskey. I dropped the handle and placed my fingers over my clit again, using two fingers to find that spot of pleasure screaming for attention. I focused on anything but sex to refrain from exploding. My fingers knew what to do without much thought, and I knew I would not win if I kept the pressure on for even a few more seconds. I pulled them away and shut off the water.

"Water's getting cold," I said, avoiding eye contact, trying to sound convincing.

"Wait, don't get out yet," he said, "One small favor?" he asked. I glanced up at him before grabbing my towel. "I want to watch you pee before you get out," he said.

"You might be in luck," I said, "I drank a ton of water during my workout today." I turned away from him and braced myself against the tiled wall. I felt the stream start immediately, working its way through my swollen lips.

"Fuck, that's hot," he said. "That's just a small sample of what is in store for us tonight. I'm going back downstairs to start dinner. You have clothes laid out for tonight's play. Love you," he said as he faded down the hall.

I quickly rinsed my legs and cunt in case there was any splatter, then stepped out and toweled off. I walked into our bedroom to find my uniform for the evening. It was a black dress comprised mainly of straps that stopped just below my crotch. Also included were red heels, a butt plug with a red heart glass tip, and a lead collar. The outfit gave me some idea of what he had planned. Nervous energy washed over me as I strapped the collar around my neck. Getting led around with a leash hooked on was not my favorite sub activity, but I also knew some of the sex acts I dreaded the most led to my greatest points of arousal. I picked up the plug and was surprised by its weight. He had laid out a heating lube, and I obeyed his wishes. As I forced it inside my ass, the heat and heaviness caused me to grab onto the dresser and take a deep breath as my body accepted the intensity of the sensation. Just when I thought I might have to remove it and tell him we needed to go down a step in plugs, the throbbing subsided enough for my confidence to return. Next, I slipped on the heels and began to feel the part. I stepped in front of our floor length mirror and knew Mr. A was going to be happy with his choices.

I found him on our deck outside, prepping the grill. I could smell potatoes baking in the oven. It was a beautiful evening. He was dressed in a pair of jeans that he filled out perfectly with a light gray dress shirt that had contrasting red sleeves, I knew to compliment my red heels and plug. He turned from the grill and drank me in with his eyes, shaking his head with approval. "You look even better than I had you pictured wearing this," he said, moving towards a bottle of red wine he had pre-selected. "Let's start with a relaxing drink. I'm not planning to ask anything from you until after dinner," he said. I relaxed a bit as I sat down with him, savoring the wine. We enjoyed a nice hour of dinner and drinks, resolving to save the clean-up for tomorrow. The sun was receding and the moon just peeking out as the air cooled. I shivered slightly, feeling the breeze against my bare arms. I moved into his lap and kissed him fully on the mouth, my tongue demonstrating my need for him. A low growl escaped his throat.

"I guess you are ready to play?" he asked, needing the final consent.

"Absolutely," I said, my cunt still throbbing with arousal, the weight of the butt plug magnifying the sensation.

"Stand up and bend over the table for inspection," he said, taking a deep breath as he transitioned into his role. I moved back to the table and put my forearms down, tits touching, legs spread wide. "Good girl," he said. "I like it when I don't have to tell you how to present yourself." He lightly caressed by butt cheeks, tugging lightly on the plug. He inserted two fingers into my cunt. "So wet already," he whispered, removing his fingers without anything more than the penetration. "Taste yourself," he instructed, placing his fingers in my mouth. I sucked on his fingers, making sure to lick all my juices off him. He placed his fingers back in my cunt, this time working them back and forth enough that I let out an involuntary gasp. He bent down to my ear and slowly gave me instructions.

"I'm going to get a fire started for us," he said. "I have set up an area to keep you on display for a while. I will use the lead to walk you down there. I expect you to pee in the yard, in a spot of my choosing, then remain on display while I work on the fire. During this time, you will not fidget or complain. Understood?" he asked.

"Yes, sir," I replied, working to please him.

"Good. Stand up," he said. I stood up from the table and he clipped a lead chain to my collar. "Let's head downstairs," He guided me down the steps, tugging slightly on the chain. I wasn't the most comfortable in heels, and I concentrated to not wobble or slip as we descended. The plug rubbed against the sensitive skin between the folds of my ass cheeks. He paused as he reached the bottom of the stairs, and I looked around the yard. I saw our small step stool that I used to reach the top cabinets sitting at the far point of the yard, away from our hot tub. He smiled as he followed my eyes to the spot. Without words, he tugged lightly on the lead and started walking towards the stool but hugging the perimeter of the property. He moved slowly, knowing I struggled in the heels. The yard was fairly firm, but I struggled several times as a heel would dip into the earth. After what seemed an eternity, we reached the stool.

I scanned outside the yard, trying to reassure myself that

we were private, even though I could hear our neighbors

enjoying the peaceful evening. He sat on the stool, his eyes

level with my crotch. He inched my dress up to uncover my

bare cunt and eased my legs apart with his hands as he

placed his mouth over my lower lips, taking his time to

explore every spot but the one spot he knew would send me

over. After just a few seconds, he pulled away and looked

up.

      "Delicious," he said, "But too soon. This is where

you are going to pee again for me. I don't want to be

standing across the room watching with your face turned

away. I am going to sit on this stool and watch from inches

away. If you can't do it right now, three things will happen.

One, you will get your first spanking of the evening, on this

stool. Two, you will take a shot of whiskey to help ease

your inhibitions, and three, you will take off that dress and do a walk of shame around the yard while I watch from this stool. But first, I'm going to go offer a shot of whiskey and have you suck on me while you are getting your mind focused on your task." He poured me a shot and traded me places. I threw back the whiskey, feeling it warm my insides immediately. I definitely needed some encouragement. I sat on the stool as he unzipped his jeans and removed his hard cock. I welcomed the distraction and went to work on it, starting by taking the full length of his cock into my mouth, focusing on not gagging as the tip of his head reached the back of my throat. I pumped him in and out of my mouth a few times before slowing to lick every inch, controlling the pace by holding his ass cheeks. He moaned approval as I found one of his balls and suckled it before devouring his cock again. He pulled away and zipped back up, taking a deep breath.

"That's enough for now; I am excited to watch you piss on the ground," he said, helping me off the stool as he sat back down. He took out his phone and set a timer. "One

minute," he said, "Good luck."

I stood before him and rolled my eyes back,

annoyed that I was being timed. I couldn't focus on the

task; I had not thought about it as I was sucking him. I

willed myself to squeeze down there, but all I felt was the

plug responding. There'd be even bigger consequences if I

squeezed it out. In no time at all, the timer chimed. He

smiled up at me and motioned for me to place myself over

his lap. I awkwardly bent over his lap. He anchored himself

by tugging down a section of the dress's leather straps and

finding a breast to hold. He spoke quietly as his hand

caressed my breast, lightly tugging at my nipple. "I don't

think you tried very hard," he said. "I also think you also

eye-rolled me earlier, so I'm going to make these sting. Do

not flex those beautiful ass cheeks."

I remained silent, waiting for the first hit. He

stroked my cheeks a moment, assessing where to start

before pulling his hand back and smacking hard across the left cheek, pausing a moment before smacking back down, three more times on the same side. I took deep breaths, focusing on not tensing. He paused another moment before striking the right cheek, then hitting just above the plug. I flexed as I felt the sting between my legs. He paused and clamped down harder on my nipple.

"No flexing," he reminded me. You have a few more blows to get your ass a nice shade of red that I can see as you walk around this yard again." I took another intake of breath as he smacked again just above the plug. I could sense his satisfaction as I willed my ass to relax. He delivered a few more blows to each cheek and rested, satisfied with the mosaic pattern of red he had created.

"I won't give you the satisfaction of finger fucking you right now," he said. "I know you are desperate to have anything in your cunt, and I won't give it to you yet. Right now, you are being punished. I instructed you to pee, and you didn't. Take another shot of whiskey," he commanded.

I happily threw back the second shot, hoping it would help

me to not cum the first time anything grazed my clit.

"Good," he said, taking a pull from the bottle. "Remove the

dress, and start walking."

I glanced around, reassuring myself it was still safe.

The moon was out fully now, the sun completely gone. As I

pulled off the dress, I felt the air against the sting of my hot

cheeks. My cunt dripped with yearning. I could feel the

wetness of my thighs. I knew the walk would go slow with

the high heels. I started walking, aware of his eyes on my

backside. I watched him as I turned the corner, knew he

was enjoying every second of my discomfort. By the time I

reached him again, I could feel the fullness of my bladder.

"I am going to offer you another shot before you try

again," he said, holding out the bottle. I followed his cue

and took a quick sip from the bottle, hoping it was enough

to help with my performance anxiety. Still sitting on the

stool, he motioned for me to stand in front of him, now fully naked, my crotch so close, I knew he'd be able to smell my urine if I could let it flow. I took a deep breath as he started the timer. One breath, two breaths, then instead of squeezing, I allowed my groin to completely relax and felt the first pulse of urine reach my lips. I squatted very slightly to separate my lips and let the stream flow, keeping my eyes closed. After a few seconds, I felt his fingers press against my cunt and the flow stopped.

"Don't stop," he said, "I want to feel the piss come out of you." I closed my eyes again and worked to not think about this hand resting now just below my crotch. The urgency of my bladder's needs took over and the piss flooded out of me. The relief was so great, I moaned as if he were touching me. As I finished, he pulled me to him and kissed me passionately. "Such a good girl," he said, wiping his hand off with a towel. "I'm going to put the lead back on you and walk you over to the fire pit. I want you to be on display while I make us a fire," he said as he hooked the lead back onto my collar and motioned for me to get up and start walking the edge of the yard. I was mostly dry but was aware of not being able to wipe myself. Mr. A had created a platform by covering a bale of straw with a heavy blanket. It was close to the fire, but not dangerously close. We kept lawn chairs by the pit, and he arranged them on both sides of the hay bale. Our hot tub and outdoor shower were also close, and I glanced over, wishing I could rinse off before being displayed.

"Hop up here and get on all fours," he instructed. I obeyed, keeping my head bent down.

"I am going to get the fire going. You are expected to stay still, not move, and not fidget. When I'm ready, I will inspect you," he said. I kept my head down but could see him moving to start the fire. He had everything ready to go, and basically needed to simply light it. I didn't anticipate him being gone so long. In a matter of minutes, I could feel the warmth of the fire but could no longer see Mr. A or hear him. Music was playing softly from our outdoor speakers. I glanced up and looked around for just a moment. Mr. A was sitting in a lawn chair by the fire, drinking a beer, staring at me, a smile on his face. I jerked my head back down, knowing I had broken a rule. Several minutes crawled by as I remained on my hands and knees, head down. I tried to discreetly shift my weight around to take some pressure off my knees. Finally, I felt Mr. A's presence. He gently massaged my ass cheeks and stroked the backs of my legs. He was standing very close to me, and I hoped he couldn't smell and drops of urine dried to my legs.

"You seem to be a little squirmy tonight," he said. I didn't respond and kept my head down. He walked around and stroked my hair, tilting my head towards him. He bent to kiss me, a small reassurance that he approved. He lightly touched each breast and nipple, then put pressure on my right nipple, pulled on it with light pressure and added a nipple clamp to it, then clamped the left nipple. The clamps felt heavy, and my nipples began to burn slightly. He unzipped his pants and pulled out his cock.

"Suck me for just a bit, no hands," he ordered. I took in his cock and started bringing him in and out of my mouth, keeping my hands on the hay bale. I slowed and focused on the tip of his penis, varying the pressure of my mouth, then sucked him all the way back in my mouth, gagging slightly and its depth. He pulled back out and zipped up.

"That's good for now," he said. "Remove your butt plug," he said next, "And put it in your mouth. Then take this beer bottle and fuck your ass with it while I drink a second beer." I glanced at the bottle. It was only half gone.

"You want me to put a half-full beer bottle in my ass and fuck it?" I asked, skeptically.

"That is what I instructed," he said. "Get the plug out so I can hand you the bottle," he said, his voice full of authority. I reached from behind and hesitated a second to put it in my mouth. Neither of these tasks were appealing to me. I didn't want to taste myself, and I didn't like the idea of beer in my asshole. I took the plug in my mouth, trying to hold in as loose as possible.

"I'm sensing some attitude," he said, shaking his head and placing the bottle carefully on the ground. He walked toward my backside and stood to the side where he was able to grab one in my breasts, cupping it with the clamp, while raising his hand back and striking my ass with a resounding slap. I jumped slightly and he applied pressure to the nipple below the clamp. Another smack came down on the other cheek. He wasn't holding back as each smack of his hand connected with my tender ass. He kept his rhythm steady and didn't let up for a dozen smacks. Each time I winced, he squeezed my nipple harder. Finally, he stopped, by ass as hot as my nipples.

He bent down and whispered in my ear. "Are you ready to fuck your ass with this bottle? Just nod yes or no."

I nodded yes and reached with one hand to take the bottle. He walked around to my ass and assisted getting the angle right.

"That is beautiful," he said, before moving away. "I'm moving my chair to get a full view of your ass." I was reluctant at first as I pulled the bottle in and out. I could feel the beer running inside my ass. It was creating a deep warmth inside me, not quite burning, but definitely a new sensation. The smooth glass of the bottle moved easily in and out and I was getting excited. I knew Mr. A was enjoying the view. I could feel my ass cheeks burning around the bottle, magnified by the contrast of the fire's warmth from one side, and the cool breeze from the other side. All my senses were responding, creating a growing swelling in my cunt. I felt wetness trickle down my thigh. I heard Mr. A get up and walk towards me. He took the plug from my mouth and put it in his pocket, then took control of the bottle.

"Play with your clit," he said, immediately pressing the bottle a bit deeper than I had allowed it to go.

"Can I cum if I'm ready?" I asked, knowing I was beyond close.

"Please do."

I started by placing two fingers in my dripping cunt, felt the bottle on the other side. It created an extra tightness to my swollen cunt. My fingers easily found my clit, at this point hyper-sensitive, and rubbed lightly. Mr. A moved to my side, keeping the bottle firmly in my ass as he unclamped one nipple and gently squeezed on it. The squeeze sent my clit into immediate overdrive and I exploded over my hand, keeping the rhythm going as I tried to not cry out so loud that neighbors might hear.

Mr. A removed the bottle but said, "Don't stop playing with yourself." I heard him unzip his pants, expecting his cock to slide into my ass. Instead, I felt a warm flow over my back, over my ass, and down my legs. I could smell his piss as he walked around me, marking his territory. I kept rubbing myself and a new wave of pleasure washed over me.

Mr. A stopped in front of my face. "Put your hand back down," he said, "Suck the piss off my cock." He moved his cock into my mouth, and I obeyed, sucking him deeply, caught up in my own desire. He pulled out abruptly and moved to my backside, entering my cunt. Holding my hips, he fucked me hard, thrusting deeply each time.

"Ask me to put it in your ass," he ordered, still pumping into my cunt.

"Fuck my ass. Please fuck my ass," I said, meaning the request. He pulled out of my cunt and slid it easily into my ass. The pleasure was immediate, and he was unapologetic as he rammed hard, letting go of hours of sexual arousal. He came hard and deeply into my ass. We remained conjoined for a few moments, both savoring the moment. He lightly stroked the red streaks on my ass and kissed them once he pulled out. Both satisfied, I knew our play session was officially over and the remainder of the evening would be spent relaxing in our hot tub by the fire.

"You might want to move your chair to face the shower," I said, "I need a quick rinse before I join you at the fire." I stepped into the water, rinsing off our mess. I glanced over and saw his smile of approval. My cunt flexed immediately, and I smiled back, hopeful we'd get in a second round before bedtime.